Another Mother's Child

Another Mother's Child

For wishes

Mary

MARY McCLAREY

Collingwood Publishing and Media Ltd,
Cheldon, Challaborough,
Kingsbridge
TQ7 4JB

ISBN 978-1-9996359-4-7

British Library Cataloguing in Publication Data.
A catalogue record for this book is available from the British Library.

Typeset in the United Kingdom by Indie-Go
https://www.indie-go.co.uk

Dedicated to the memory of Granny,
Kathleen (Kitty) Cahalane.

Denoting only main
characters that feature in
Another Mother's Child

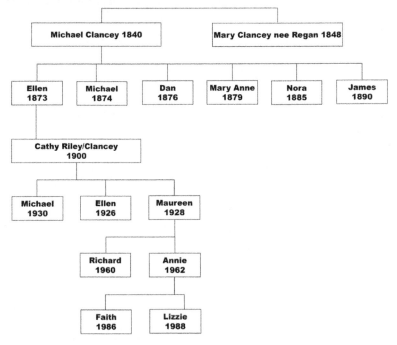

| Michael Clancey 1840 | Mary Clancey nee Regan 1848 |

| Ellen 1873 | Michael 1874 | Dan 1876 | Mary Anne 1879 | Nora 1885 | James 1890 |

Cathy Riley/Clancey
1900

| Michael 1930 | Ellen 1926 | Maureen 1928 |

| Richard 1960 | Annie 1962 |

| Faith 1986 | Lizzie 1988 |

Contents

Chapter 1

Ellen. West Cork: July 1900.

A weak Irish sun, having lost its midday shine, was beginning to dull the banks and lanes around the West Cork countryside and a waning heat was leaving halfway through the afternoon.

The fields had seen no rain for weeks and dry mud caked the lane leading up to the farmhouse. As the soil hardened and cracked it cemented into deep ruts, a legacy of the winter's horse and cart troughs on either side.

Deep ruts meant Ellen Clancey needed to pull her boots out of the laundry basket she'd been balancing on her hip, before she could walk down the lane. Hopping and jigging from foot to foot, she concentrated on gripping the overfull container, whilst pushing her feet into the dry aged leather. And it helped keep her mind off the other thing.

Her ankle-length skirt flapped against the boots, giving a rhythm to her steps, and she puffed in time to the hop-flap-hold-hop rhythm until she reached home.

Resting her load on the low stone wall bounding the cobbled yard, which framed a slender white farmhouse, she straightened her skirt. Slowing her breathing to a regular pace, she gave voice to her anger.

'Years, I've had of it, years of obedience, and here I am, twenty-six, domestic servant, that's what they call me at Lahana House. Servant, always the servant, at home or over there. Soon everyone will know I let them down. Shown them what I really was. After all this time of doing whatever they expected, they'll be shocked. Oh yes, our Ellie, always had to be responsible, no matter what age.'

Looking towards the open door, she saw the outline of a tall, wide-hipped woman, swaddled in an apron. She was stepping and dipping around inside with quick, busy movements.

Ellen had watched this woman, her mother, resentfully groan out the sixth child, James, now called Jimmy, as though the baby was one more burden. The maternal flush which ran through Ellen when they handed her the child had been a surprise. The first person to hold the baby, she had been witness on his birth register and every time she saw him she recalled the warm dampness of his newborn smell.

As she thought the word, "Mother," it came back and slapped her in the face. Stinging. "Mother Church," "Mother Ireland," "Mother of God," "Mother." What was she expected to be now, she wondered?

A mother loves, cares and makes decisions. She protects and teaches and is always there. A mother is not someone who concentrates on hopping down a lane so she doesn't have to think about the other thing.

Her child. It. That wasn't a word she was ready to use for the slight swelling in her belly. Ellen had managed to ignore the hard, full heat-tingling in her breasts and the constant urge in her bladder.

No, she reckoned, it was something else had delayed the curse since Easter, four missed now. But she'd heard that worry could do that. And there had been no sickness, she'd not been even a bit off her food. That was unusual. So maybe it really was the best thing to do. She'd put it out of her mind for a while, no need to go in there worrying them all for nothing.

Having made a decision and rested her limbs, she lifted the heavy basket off the wall and onto her other hip. Sighing, she pushed the anxiety aside, downgrading it, giving it a lower place on her waiting list of worries. She let her eyes wander across the stones. They patchworked the farmyard, grey and smooth, worn by donkeys, horses and people, as familiar to her as her own body. She thought their curves, chips and hollows told a tale of her family over many generations. She chewed her lower lip, wondering what her own impact on them might look like in years to come.

The family had needed donkeys to fetch and carry. The sound of their hooves, as they clopped across the cobbles, had always rung out the working day. Dainty steps, fine-boned legs out of proportion to their fat bellies, marked time in an unchanging rhythm. Now the family had a horse, the barest suggestion that they were no longer subsisting but edging towards security.

'We were never the family with the money. Donkeys and carts, that was us and now we're hopin' for a bit more. But not me, clumsy fool that I am. Not one for expectin' too much attention at the cross-roads now.'

Shaking her head, Ellen feared her future would be, at best, lacklustre. She considered that the plait of thick hair, mahogany dark, which snaked down past her shoulders, summed up her lack of style or glamour. Looking across the yard she watched Jimmy, now an independent ten-year-old, trudge out of the lean-to barn. He carried the horse rope and bit over his shoulder.

He was the slightest built of the Clanceys, with a great tussle of dark red hair, a pale face and a nature which avoided a quarrel at all costs. Her favourite, the baby. He glanced across at her, and nodded. His narrow deep-set blue eyes lighting up just for a flicker, she knew he was not one to show emotion.

'Jimmy boy, come on over here and tell me all the craic. Were ye at school the day? How'd it go?'

'I was so, but I'll leave soon. Not soon enough for Dada. I'd need to be bringing in some money, an' sure they all say I'll never make a scholar.'

A deep throated, impatient voice interrupted. 'Come on in

Ellie girl, and be bringing in that laundry. We're waiting on it so we are.'

Ellen looked across at Jim, her smile tinged with concern. Seeing him there and wanting his company, she recalled how he'd been as a small child. As if it was yesterday. He'd crouch down in the cobbled yard, scratching the dried chicken guano around the scrawny birds with a stick. She thought she had really tried to be like a mother to him. For sure, being present at his birth had started it, but she'd also looked after him when Mammy, Mother – that word again – was recovering. Or, while Mammy was too busy, or when Mammy was tired.

She expected that the power of the bond she had with Jimmy would always be important to her, central to her comfort, always one to worry about. He was the first one to call her Sissie, and now her brothers and sisters did too. 'Up, carry up, Sissie.' She remembered the pale skinny arms raised high, bony wrists shooting out from the sleeve of a handknit jumper. Scratchy purple wool. How long, she asked herself, had it had taken to knit? And long enough again it had been unravelling the wool from one of the older boys' worn out sweaters.

She used to be able to lift him onto her hip, kissing the grubby head and waiting for his knees and elbows to anchor themselves against her. Now he was half-grown and defensive, like a boy who wants to be a man.

'Leaving school already?'

'Can't wait. I'll get some freedom then so I will, an' fish an' ride out an' no schoolmaster tellin' me what to do.'

Slipping through the gate-gap in the stone wall, ignoring the command coming from inside the house, Ellen changed her tone. She spoke with authority, sounding more like the schoolteacher he was so keen to escape.

'You'll never get a chance to better yourself if you leave now, Jimmy. Look me in the eye and tell me it's really what you want.'

4

'I've no choice, Sissie. We need the money and I can get plenty of farm work. Sure they won't be requiring book learning.'

'You will never be better than they are, tenant farmer at best, probably not even that. You'll end up in a tied cottage, working to the gentry every day, coming home with a pittance and no way out of it. I'm a servant, that's bad enough, but you, you'll be a slave.'

A shadow fell across the yard, shading Jim's worried face.

'Now Ellie, what's keepin' ye girl? I'm sick calling an' there's a mountain of work to be finished yet before the milking.'

Her mother, red-faced, stood firm, with no suggestion that a delay would be possible. Hands on her hips and feet planted wide across the doorway.

'Coming Mam, just having a word with our Jimmy.'

'Now girl, ye great lump, get yersel' over with the basket before I run out of patience.'

Turning away from the boy, Ellen dawdled across the yard, not disobeying, just keeping a small amount of control. Her eyes took a moment to adjust to the dark interior as she entered the main room. A low smoking fireplace glowed on one side and there was an uneven tread to the floor.

Two small, tax-avoiding windows, paned with thick crusty glass, allowed just enough light for work, but not enough for leisure. She knew their house was better than many in the area, with separate sleeping and living areas. Close sharing was an uncomfortable fact she'd got used to as the family had expanded.

Ellen dumped the basket near the edge of the table, not wanting to take the space her mother used for baking. She pushed a wooden bench aside, creating a gap where she could sit down, readying herself for the unpleasant task ahead. She hated washing other people's clothes, sorting through the sticky bits, trying not to think about who had worn them, or where the stains came from.

'I didn't eat today Ma, no cold cuts around and the maid's breakfast was over by the time I got back from collecting up the washing. Is there anything in the pot to be going on with?'

'Sort those into piles Ellie, I'll begin with the soaking, then you can take an early tea. I've it nearly ready, take it before the men come in so you're sure to get enough. I'm thinkin' ye maybe need it. Now tell me. Since your wash has been scrubbed alongside theirs, I've not seen any rags soaked this month an' I don't recall seeing any last month either. What ails ye, girl?'

Ellie bent her head over the sour smelling heap of garments she'd tipped onto the table, intent on pulling out the finer, more delicate cuffs, nightgowns and collars. They would need careful washing and repair, kept apart from the heavier soiled shirts, breeches and pinafores.

'Nothing Ma, it's nothing. Just a bit late, that's all.'

'How late, girl? How late?'

Ellen looked up and saw surprise, disbelief and then shock flit like clouds on a windy day, across her mother's face. Her coarse features softened and the ruddy complexion paled.

'Who is it girl, has taken advantage of ye? Who is he?'

'Ma don't get ahead of yourself now, please. Only missed a few months, haven't been sick or anything like that. I wasn't going to say anything, not worry ye like.'

Her mother was the taller and stronger of the two. Ellen was in awe of her broad, muscular frame, developed by haymaking, potato gathering and animal husbandry. But her mother had told them all how she'd also been one of the lucky ones. When only the strongest children survived the famine years, for the rest of their lives they approached the world as a challenge. Mary Clancey always met her challenges head on.

Now she pulled her daughter to standing, cupping her elbow with one hand whilst the other searched, running up and down over her belly before stopping at a full hard breast and giving it a slight squeeze. Ellen bit her lip and winced.

'Open your bodice girl, let me see.'

Ellen's fingers shook as she unpicked the laces, which she had had to slacken recently and let the front of her bodice gape. Hoping to avoid more probing, she pulled her vest out from under the bodice, showing her left breast. It was full and hard but what drew a sharp intake of breath from her mother was the sight of the darkened prominent nipple.

She heard a noise at the door, stamping boots on the hard-packed earth of the floor. Her younger brother, Dan, who'd been cutting hay with their neighbour Patrick, pushed the door open. His eyes widened as he took in the unusual scene of his sister half undressed.

'Get out boy, give us peace here for a minute.' Dan's embarrassed sniff, rapidly followed by a sharp pull of the door, filled Ellen with shame. Her body heated with her mother's handling and her brother's response.

Mary Clancey watched, her face paled and serious, waiting until Ellen had readjusted her clothing and relaced her bodice. 'I'll ask you girl, who is he?'

'Why Ma, what is it you've seen? Is there something wrong with me?'

'There is indeed something wrong. You are with child and no doubt about it. These are the changes, never mind about the sickness. I think maybe you're past that stage now anyway.

So who, girl? Don't make me slap you, not in the state you're in.'

'No, Ma. I've no want of a child. I didn't know it would happen like it did. It wasn't my fault, I didn't mean it and now what can I do?'

'Who?' Her mother stood back, giving Ellen space to wipe her damp face, her body quivering as she leaned against the side of the table for support.

She thought of the times she'd spent with young Tom Berish, Landlord Tom Berish's son, from Lahana House. The times he'd taken her out riding on the back of his horse. She'd loved that, and knew how to handle horses. She felt his equal. She hadn't felt his equal though when he'd laid on top of her, covering her mouth with kisses while he fumbled with her undergarments. And then, the exciting sensation when he'd entered her. After the first couple of times she'd trembled with anticipation when she thought about the pleasure.

She had missed his attention when he stopped following her around, surprising her with a kiss and a compliment every few days. She knew now that the afternoons they had spent together were the cause of her child, and she'd have to think quickly. Without too much forethought, it felt easier to lie to her mother than to explain the truth.

'I'd say it's Patrick alright. Patrick Riley, so it is. An' I've no wish to discuss it any further.'

'You've no wish, girl? Well that's neither here nor there now. Discuss it you'll be doing and the sooner the better too.'

Turning towards the fireplace she lifted a bowl from the shelf above and half filled it with a steaming broth. The colour began to return to her face and as she handed the bowl to Ellen. she pulled the bench closer, taking her shaking daughter by the elbow, sitting beside her and nodding for her to eat.

'Get that down ye now girl, and soon as you're done go out and get Patrick. Bring him in to me and he'll see your father later.

Ellen stomped down the lane, boots pulled on at the door and no heed taken stepping around the ruts. She marched across the road, then down the valley and over the brook. She slowed, stopping to draw a breath, just before reaching the dip in the fields. Screwing her eyes she glimpsed the mouldy, patched, thatched roof of the Riley family's tiny cabin.

Checking there was no one in sight, she sat on a large boulder, bunching her full skirts under her thighs. It took her a few moments to clarify her thoughts and plan. One conversation now, she told herself, then there'd be no going back. What should she say, she wondered, what could she say to persuade him?

'Sure he is only a lad, an agricultural labourer, with no means whatever an' not likely to be gettin' any in the future,' she muttered, rubbing her feet back and fore in the dry ground, hoping by voicing her plan it would make it sound more plausible. 'An' I'm right sorry to do this to ye' Patrick. I like ye well enough, always give me a dance at the cross-roads, so ye do. But any dope would know, this wasn't the result of a dance at the cross-roads.'

Shaking her head, feeling the thick rope of her plait swishing back and forth across her shoulders she looked up at the sky, its mauve light fading.

'But what else can I do? Will I be left alone with a baby? Well I'll starve then, or maybe the workhouse – or will I just die? There won't be any work for me as a servant. It's all I'm trained for, but not with a baby alongside and certainly not over there.' Ellen didn't expect the Berishes to be lenient.

She considered what she'd heard of their reputation amongst the tenant farmers. It was reckoned that Landlord Tom never gave second chances and his wife was just as tough. 'Ah, the lady now, she's my only hope. Will it be worth taking on the cause of a kitchen servant to cover up the truth? 'Tis a chance I'll take alright.'

Closing her eyes, which she'd always found made concentration a lot easier, she considered her options. She knew that if she didn't get her story straight and secure now, she'd have to live with the scandal, like Ann Maher. She recalled how that had shocked everyone.

'The poor girl, barely twenty, sent to prison. Two years she got. For killing her baby. Well, I do pity her, no man to give his name or support the child, but to leave her little boy, its tiny white body, in a manure pit, that was harsh.'

Ellen had read the newspaper report aloud to her parents; it was printed in English and they were Irish speakers. As the newspaper serialized the events over the weeks, she'd been pleased to see a growing sympathy for Ann Maher. The desperation of the girl, when nowhere would take the child in, none of the workhouses she approached or the orphanages. Her mam had said that that was Dublin for you, of course. She reckoned Cork was a kinder county altogether, which, Ellen thought, remained to be seen.

Her plan began to take shape as the jumble of ideas cleared. She'd go to Lahana House, see Lady Berish herself, before speaking to Patrick. She reckoned Dada would just have to wait. There'd be no benefit in telling young Tom, or his father.

She knew Landlord Berish was not a man to show consideration or weakness of any kind. He was set against the tenant farmers owning their own land, angered by the success of their campaign to reduce the rack rents. Listening to the men talking by the fire when they came visiting of an evening, it seemed that all around the country there were ongoing problems. Some tenant farmers still faced eviction, unable to pay even a reduced rent when there was a poor harvest. Dada said Landlord Tom was a cruel man, with no compassion.

She knew her father and brothers were amongst the fortunate ones who held a lease of 'Three Lives' for their land. She winced, recalling the terms of the lease. It meant three generations, and she'd seen how a life was expected to range from twenty one years to thirty one years, before the individual 'dropped'. She'd felt a flush of insult when she'd read those words on the farm's papers, so disrespectful. To have used that word when an animal calved, 'a cow dropped', that was fine alright. But it was wrong to say such a thing when the life of a human being expired. She promised herself she'd never write or speak such words to mean a human death.

'Well, I'm a scholar myself, they wrote it on the census, schooled in both Irish and English. So I'm not stupid. I can do this and come out the better of it.'

She sat on a moment longer, savouring the quiet, aware that a confrontation was waiting.

The landlord certainly was a very unpopular man. She remembered rumours of his misfortunes, recounted with glee. He'd lost a herd of two-year-old cattle "through a gap in the hedge" one night. They vanished, and now, the man himself took to parading the grounds at night with his musket loaded. He would not be slow at using firearms. 'An' he'd evict quick as look at ye,' she'd heard one man tell Dada. 'A different kettle of fish altogether from his father, Dick. He never put a farmer on the road.'

She knew it wasn't as bad as the tales she'd heard about the famine. People weren't starving on the roadsides in their hundreds, but there were families having difficulty. Paying rent often meant that food became scarce. The landlord was a magistrate too, he'd plenty of power to throw around.

Then there was the story about 'boycotting', the practice of cutting out any farmer who took the land from an evicted family. Her father said they were "landgrabbers," and no blacksmith would shoe the horse or merchant buy stock from such a man. He'd told them that once, when a "landgrabber" had actually shown their face in the church, the congregation got up and left. That was a tough penalty alright.

'An' what will be my penalty, I wonder? Will I be avoided an' disgraced? Funny how this all feels more real now than it did this morning.' She rubbed the back of her hand across her forehead, as though to push the idea away. Twitching her mouth at one corner she pulled a reed from the soggy mud around her boulder seat.

'No baby this morning, just a bit late and so on. An' now Mam has decided that's what it will be. I don't want it, I'm scared. I want things to be just the way they were. Me at the big house five days a week, and a pound for three months. An' whatever feed I get, sometimes it's not all bad.'

Ellen sighed. 'I like the company, the rest of us servants, the blacksmith and stableboys. Not have Ma at me all day. The only reason I come home now is for Jimmy. Sure he's enough of a baby for me. As for Patrick Riley, well, he's something else altogether, hasn't a farthing to his name. I need to gather mesel' together now so I do, an' see what help is to be had.'

She pulled the reed apart with her thumbnails, picking out the soft white inside and scraping at the stem as it shredded. Her back ached and she saw that damp seeping through the moss had marked her skirt.

Brushing the shredded reeds off her lap, she picked her way across the fields towards the imposing stone building which dominated the skyline. Someone had told her that the house was around one hundred and fifty years old, but she'd shrugged, uninterested in the lives of the gentry. They were only employers, a means to an end, and she'd long ago decided to live in the here and now. Her feelings were much more for those who earned their living from the estate.

She knew Lahana had been established long before there were any cabins, cottages and farmsteads. The countryside was scattered with small, single storey dwellings, like lambs in a field and she expected that would never change.

The house was different from the surrounding buildings. Standing proud, dominating the area, three stories high. The wide wooden doorway was framed by stone pillars on either side and the whole building was topped by a heavy slate roof. The roof itself supported by beams of bog oak. She'd admired those beams from the inside, all hewn by tenants, labourers who wouldn't consider using bog oak to build their own homes.

She smiled at the thought of a cabin needing such support. No cottage or even farmhouse like the Clancey's used such solid, long lasting materials.

'Oh, they'll last here alright,' she muttered, approaching the house across the wide gravel driveway. 'No ruts on this lane, nor uprisings, riots or famine. It'll always be the same, landlords, overseers and tenant farmers. They'll go on forever, so they will.'

Ellen knew every windowpane and sill of the house, reckoning she'd cleaned most of them. Approaching the red front door, she wiped her hands against the rough serge of her skirt.

Her nose wrinkled as she considered how time spent shredding reeds and sitting on the damp mossy boulder might not have been a good idea. She looked down at her trailing hem seeping a damp brown residue and chided herself for appearing end-of-day scruffy. Licking her dry lips, she pushed away a few loose strands of hair which had fallen over her eyes. She took a deep breath and climbed the wide stone steps which led up to the substantial wooden front door.

Ellen's more than medium height wasn't enough to prevent her from stretching to reach the heavy brass door-knocker. The threatening sound it made on impact against its hitter took her by surprise. It seemed to echo outside and around the walls, fierce and confident. Her knees shook and she fought with her legs, persuading them not to turn around. She'd only ever heard the door-knocker sound from inside although she'd never opened the door, that was the job of the upper servants.

She could hear a scuttling noise, which she thought would probably be Hannah Daley the parlour maid, wrestling with the bolts. She braced herself, knowing that now there could be no turning back. The dense wooden panelling swung slowly inward, and as the hinges creaked, Ellen made a note to tell her brother Michael. He'd recently been promoted to butler and he'd be seen in a good light with the housekeeper if he oiled the hinges unasked.

A small pale face, the colour of ash bark, appeared at the door and its owner stepped back, startled, her grey narrow eyes widening.

'What're ye thinkin', Ellie? Use the back door an' get away before yer seen.'

Hannah's dun coloured pinafore, although now day-long and ready for a change of apron, looked fresher than Ellen's muddied skirt and wrinkled blouse. Ignoring Hannah's groomed appearance, although it had made her heart sink and her cheeks flush, Ellen stood tall, upright, head held high. That brought her a couple of inches above Hannah. Being able to look down made her feel she had a slight edge.

'No, this is the door I need, Hannah. Please tell Lady Berish I'm here. I'll wait.'

'Are ye daft or what? She'll never see ye. She's gettin' dressed for dinner anyway.'

'I said tell her I'll wait. I'm here now and she should know why.'

Hannah shrugged her shoulders and disappeared into the gloom of the hallway, its black flagstones catching a glimmer of light from the open door. When Ellen worked around the house there was always plenty of light coming from the arched lobby window and the three upper dormer ones. She hadn't wondered, until now, what time the candles would be lit.

Her small pool of confidence seeped away as she realised how little she really knew of life within the house. She spoke aloud to herself, suggesting more courage than she felt.

'Perhaps I will be called a fool, in my condition, to risk losing the only chance of a living. Well, I'll not beg or fall to the poorhouse, and I'll keep my head and get what I came for, so I will.'

The minutes stretched, the wait dragged its heels. She pushed the toe of her boot into the front doorsill, ignoring the screaming inside that urged her to turn around and run. Eventually she heard the high English voice of Lady Berish, berating Hannah for leaving the front door open. 'Anyone could have come in and stolen, broken in or just defiled. Yes, de-filed. That's what they might have done. You've no thought to your master's property, have you Hannah, no thought at all. You people, you're all the same.'

The sound of swishing skirts on flagstones gave Ellen time to clear her throat, ready to speak.

Avril Berish stood before her, wrapped in pale silk. She thought her silver grey dress and the softly shining cream pearls around her neck made her far removed from Ellen's world. "Rather like a pouting pigeon, with that corset throwing her chest forward as her hips strained back. What must that feel like?" she wondered, shifting comfortably in her loose skirt and recently re-tied bodice.

She had seen Lady Berish around the house many times. She was usually dressed in tough fabrics, tweed or linen, giving the housekeeper instructions, or in riding clothes waiting for her horse to be brought around to the front for a day's hunting.

And once, last autumn, when everyone had had to work late, nearly the whole night, there had been the hunt ball. Ellen had seen them all, the glittering headwear and the men in long tailed coats. She'd considered then that it had been well worth the late night just for the sights. She loved to see the style and shenanigans of the gentry. Lost in her thoughts, she startled when she heard Lady Berish's voice.

'What can you be thinking? A servant, I am sure I have seen you around the kitchen, arriving here uninvited and interrupting us at this time of the evening. I'm getting ready for dinner and the master will soon be home.'

'I need to speak with you Lady Berish, it's private so it is.'

Avril Berish's head drew back. Either contaminated by the words or attempting to strengthen her pigeon-like approach, it was impossible to tell. But the combination of both options gave Ellen the courage to continue.

'It's private, Milady.' She was repeating herself, but Hannah was still standing behind. She appeared to be waiting to hear what brought Ellen Clancey, a kitchen servant, to the front door.

'Fine. Hannah, you can leave us now.' Hannah moved reluctantly away, barely out of sight. 'Whatever can you and I have in common which might be private?'

'I'm Ellen Clancey, Milady. I live over at Derreena with my family..'

'And?'

'Well, ye see, it's delicate. Tom, young Master Tom, that is. He, well he likes me see, an' I like him too.'

Lady Berish's brow furrowed, her colour rose a small degree and her lips seemed to pluck themselves tightly together as her nostrils flared. Now she looked, to Ellen, more like one of the estate's thoroughbred horses about to join the hunt than a pigeon.

'I'm afraid, young woman, I've never heard him mention you. I very much doubt he'd want to either. But so very grateful to you for letting me know. Now, is that all?'

'No, Milady. There's to be a baby.'

'Well, it's certainly not anything to do with my son, that I can assure you. Now be off, you've kept me late already.'

'I won't go 'til I'm seen to then. I'll just stay here on the doorstep and see as he comes or maybe see the master when he gets back. I'll tell him the same.'

The furrow on Avril Berish's brow deepened. Ellen stood firm, hoping there was a chance that she'd be offered something. She also knew Lady Berish would have to have time to consider.

She reckoned the mistress would probably speak to her son, and then make up her own mind about the risk of rumour. It wasn't a house which shielded its business from the servants and everyone overheard family arguments.

Michael had told her that Tom was already on a warning from his father, his gambling was getting out of control. He'd also said there was a young servant who had taken Tom's eye last year. She'd left in a hurry. Apparently the girl hadn't seemed too unhappy as her family had taken her in, and kept her child, along with a new set of horses.

Tom was a charmer, she would admit that to anyone and she'd enjoyed the time when he'd pestered, flattered and followed her. She'd always known it wouldn't become anything. It was an amusement for him and she did like a bit of fun too. But this wasn't fun, and she needed help.

'Will I stay here Milady, while you decide? I hear Lady Linehan of the Ballinvarrig estate was pleased for Tom to meet her daughter a while ago. I wouldn't want to get in the way there, not at all.'

Ellen had heard plenty of speculation amongst the staff about the negotiations. The Linehans were wealthy and although none of them thought the young woman would be keen on the match, Tom's parents were. The servants had heard him being coaxed to show some enthusiasm.

Ellen was sure that was why he hadn't sought her company for a couple of months. Of course he'd be on his best behaviour now. And he couldn't afford the rumour of a child. Even one denied might quench any flicker of interest from the Linehans.

'Tom's affairs are nothing to do with you, young woman. What did you say your name was?'

'Ellen. Ellen Clancey, Milady.'

'Well Helen, I shall speak with Tom after dinner and send for you tomorrow, sometime during your working day. I expect Hannah knows how to get you?'

'Yes Milady, I'm here from before the breakfasts, I bring the laundry up first thing.'

17

'And you'll say nothing of this conversation or of your condition until after we have spoken. Understood? Clearly? Because if I do hear a whisper you will never come near this house again, or any of the other big houses across all Ireland.'

'Yes Milady, ma'am, perfectly. Thank you. Tomorrow then.'

Lady Berish had turned away before Ellen finished speaking. She stood in the doorway until she heard Hannah's name being called, instructing her to close the door. 'Helen,' she muttered. 'I'll show her tomorrow, I'll show that woman to call me Helen.'

Chapter 2

Bristol. Lizzie: May 2022.

Heads turned as a slim, pixie-faced girl, wearing less than the weather outside demanded, weaved between crowded tables in the Wheatsheaf Bar. With a bag of crisps tucked beneath each armpit and two glasses of wine gripped against her chest, Lizzie ignored the admiring glances. She could only concentrate on reaching her table. Unable to speak because her teeth were clenched around a credit card, she plonked the drinks down in front of her companion, letting the bags of crisps tumble.

'So, what's up, Lizzie?' Rufus lounged in his seat, his tall frame rocking the chair back slightly, then bringing it back to all fours with a harsh "clunk" on the imitation marble floor. Pulling his ponytail taut, which gave his face a sculptured, fashionably androgynous appearance, he reached across the table for his drink. 'Why the mid-week date? We don't usually have an outing on a Monday. School night and all that.'

So many late night discussions about where and how and could they squeeze a bit of time. Now she was about to throw every option out the window. Yeah, Lizzie reckoned, this was going to be harsh. They were both so busy, her work and horse riding, his work, sports and photography, their mates. Managing even a few days' leave together was difficult, and now she was jettisoning any chance of a getaway.

'Mum. It's Mum, on the phone, this morning.'

'And?'

'Wants me to come home, see Granny. She's not got long and's been asking for me.'

'Well go then, what's the big deal? Fly from Bristol, you could be there and back easily over the weekend.'

'That's just it Rufie, she wants a longer visit, says she hasn't seen me in ages, and what with Granny being so ill an' all I feel I should spend some days over there. We've got holiday time booked.'

'Yup, we sure have. Or we did have eh? But I tell you what Lizzie, Northern Ireland is fine for a party, great craic for a piss-up and all. I don't think it's my holiday destination, as you know, so I'm going to pass. You go though. Ben has a spare ticket for Glastonbury, so I'll go there, take some great shots of the bands and hang out. Go. Do your fam thing, Liz, and everybody happy. No?'

'Yeah, I guess. Thanks for being so understanding anyway, I thought you might flip! When's Glasto? Next week or what?'

'June. But hey, I'll go when I go. You sort yourself out. We aren't tied at the hip. Now, shall we get some takeaway or go for dinner, or just head home?'

'Let's do takeaway, I'll organize flights tonight and let Mum know.'

A few days later, Lizzie's flight landed at Belfast's George Best Airport. She smiled at that, naming an airport after one of the city's more infamous sons. The deceased playboy footballer had a sense of humour and she felt fellow warmth for the good looking dark-haired hero. She couldn't help mumbling his words into the cashmere scarf she'd wound around her neck. '*I spent a lot of money on booze, birds and fast cars. The rest I just squandered.*' "Only Belfast could handle that," Lizzie thought.

"Like me, Belfast girl, I do seem to attract footloose men myself."

Wheeling her suitcase down the ramp, Lizzie scanned the arrivals hall for her sister. Faith, Lizzie's older sister, was always expected to do airport pickups. Lizzie felt a flash of guilt run through her. As a teacher working in Antrim, it was a forty-minute drive in traffic after a day's teaching, but her mother never considered that to be an inconvenience.

Reading her mobile phone screen, a tall, well-built woman in an oversized shabby coat was leaning against the pillar of the airport meeting point. Lizzie headed across the gleaming concourse, pulling her neck up from the cashmere depths of her scarf, widening her eyes and smiling in mock surprise.

'Long time no see, Sis.'

Faith dragged her eyes from the screen and looked at the young woman standing in front of her. She raised her eyebrows as she took in the suitcase and shiny handbag, ignoring her sister's extended arm reaching towards her in greeting.

'Oh, hi. Your flight's in then?'

'Well yes, I think that's obvious, and lovely to see you too.'

Lizzie shook her head, she hadn't meant it to come out like that. Too sharp. She recalled how they used to be close but over the years their lives had turned in different directions. Now, although only a couple of years apart, she began to wonder whether they had drifted too far.

'How's yer man?' Faith asked, pulling a set of car keys out of the pocket of a loose coat which on purchase might have been described as camel. Lizzie suspected goat. She shuddered, watching Faith shove the mobile into her pocket, reckoning she'd never load her good coat with a phone and keys.

They walked alongside one another, not together, not apart, suggesting they were one party. A passerby might assume they were business colleagues, rather than sisters who hadn't met for over a year.

'You mean Rufus? Fine, he's fine. Cancelled his holiday for this week of course. But off to Glastonbury in a few weeks with his mates, doesn't hang around, our Rufie.'

'Well, that's how you like them isn't it? No cling-ons? Didn't the last fella make that mistake an' then ye kicked him out.'

'Thanks for mentioning that, Faith. Actually, he's married now, Adam. Has a big house just outside Bath and the wife's preggers.'

'Ah, maybe a cling-on mightn't have been such a bad idea after all. Or wasn't that what you had in mind?'

'Shall I get the car park, Faith? Give me the ticket and I'll go to the machine.'

Lizzie's face flushed and the fix of her expression was no longer delighted. She swallowed, accepting that it would be fair to feel sorry for Faith. She lived with their mother, who was becoming more demanding as she got older, which cramped her sister's freedom. But, Lizzie reasoned, that didn't excuse her pick, pick, picking away at weak spots. She knew, and she knew Faith knew, that Adam had been lovely, just a bit too caring. Not exactly a cling-on but not robust enough.

She remembered once telling Faith, and later regretting doing so, that he should "grow a pair."

Rufus was exactly the opposite and the small shiver of excitement that she'd begun to expect when she thought of him pleased her. She shook her head, determined to dislodge any suggested criticism from her sister.

The two women dipped their heads as they walked across the windswept car park and were unable to talk further until they reached Faith's shiny little Fiesta. Lizzie noticed that Faith's cars, in contrast to her wardrobe, were always well maintained. Lizzie's own car, which was mostly used to get her to the stables and back, was muddy and functional. The backseats and boot messy with tack and feed.

'Been to the car wash, Faith?'

'Just for you, Liz. Come on, get in.' Faith shrugged off her coat, throwing it carelessly onto the back seat. Lizzie folded hers and laid it on top of the suitcase. Then, making sure her coat wouldn't slip onto the floor, she settled her designer handbag in the front seat next to her.

'How's Granny then?'

'On her last legs they reckon, been asking for you though. Always were her favourite, golden girl.'

'Well, she did take me in when I was a baby, when Mum was in hospital, after having you.'

'Yes, great, thanks for mentioning that, Lizzie. And I went to a baby home, no "mother and" about it.'

'Come on Faith, get over it. Mum adores you, you know she does. You are the good one, stayed home helping her get through that awful year when we were all in coronavirus lockdown. Well I'm just the lost cause living in sin with my fella, mixing with those journalist types, newspaper editors, TV stars..'

'Err, not exactly what I heard, Liz. Aren't you rather far down the pecking order in that magazine company you work for? TV stars? Well that's news to me. But for sure we all know about you and the sinning. Been going on a long time that has, shameless hussy. Slut.' The corners of Faith's mouth twisted into a downward grin, confirming that was a joke and, despite herself, Lizzie shrugged her shoulders and laughed.

Something began chirping from the back seat.

'Bloody Nora. Get that, will you?'

'Sounds like a distressed bird, Faith. What on earth?'

'It's my phone, in the coat.'

Lizzie stretched behind, fishing the phone out of Faith's pocket and reading the name on the screen.

'It's Mum.'

'Yes. I know. It's Mum's ringtone. See what's up before it cuts out, will you?'

'Hi Mum, it's me, Lizzie. Yes, great thanks, really good. On time, no problem. Oh, OK I'll ask her, she's driving. Well, no I know that. Of course, she wouldn't answer the phone if she's driving Mum, but she can speak to you through me, can't she?'

Turning to Faith and squashing the phone between her hand and her chest, Lizzie whispered, 'We should go straight to the home. Gran's really weak. Mum's there now, she'd like us to get there as soon as we can.'

Faith sighed, raised her eyebrows, and nodded.

'Yup, no worries Mum, we're on our way. What? Oh, not far from Coleraine I think, so about another half an hour or so. See you. Love you, Mum. Bye.'

'Hmm, OK what's up now, Liz? Are we going to spend the evening in the home? No sign of dinner or wine tonight then. This does happen a lot, be prepared. Between the two of them, they have me dancing around every other day. I've a nice bottle of Pinot Grigio in the fridge and I was looking forward to an evening at home and a good dinner. Mum said she was cooking.'

'Look Faith, I feel bad about it always being you who has to take them on, Mum and Granny. I know since Dad died Mum's become a bit dependent on you, although she doesn't need to be. She's not even sixty yet. But anyway, I really can't do much more than come over when she asks. Listen, I'll take you out for dinner tomorrow night. Promise. On me entirely. You say where, just the two of us.'

'I think Mum will want to come too.'

'OK just the three of us then, as long as she behaves.'

As they drove into Portrush, Lizzie watched shards of light bouncing off the stormy Atlantic Ocean, which bounded one side of the town. Sleek, rain-washed pavements reflected the dim streetlights.

'Reminds me, Faith, that although it's end of spring in Bristol, it feels like winter here.'

'Not a sign of a tourist at all either, Lizzie, you'll be the only one. Great that they keep the streets so well lit, never know when a riot might break out.'

'Drugs, sex and rock 'n' roll? In sleepy old Portrush in the rain? Probs not!'

Faith swung into a space beside a familiar blue and white logo indicating 'Roebank Nursing Home. Visitor parking'. They walked towards the front entrance of a wide, grey pebble-dashed building.

Faith keyed some numbers onto a security pad at the side of the porch and the electronic doors swung open.

'Security code? Not much security in that, is there, Faith?'

'Ah well, I'm trusted as family, this is a home after all, not a prison.'

'And the residents, how do they get out?'

'Well, of course they don't. Can't. But that is the point. Wouldn't want them parading up and down Portrush High Street in their nighties now, would we?'

'Suppose not, even without the rock 'n' roll hordes. Bit rank in here isn't it? Do I smell pee or Sudocreme?'

'Bit of both I should think, but it doesn't put them off their dinners. Granny's been eating like a horse, still skinny as a rake though. Confused at times, and at other times, clear as a bell.'

The click clack of their shoes was the only sound breaking the silence in the brightly lit corridor, its bland walls intersected by coloured stripes along both sides.

'Helps them find their way around. Blue for dining room, red for bedrooms.'

Lizzie remembered now how Faith always knew what her sister's question would be before she asked. Looking at the handrail running the length of the corridor, she attempted a joke.

'And the ballerinas? Where do they hang out?'

Faith smiled, showing her dimples, as Lizzie squeezed her sister's elbow and giggled.

They stopped in front of a bright blue door, marked 'Mrs Maureen McCormick'.

'Why the doorknocker and letterbox, for goodness' sake? If that's an attempt to make this seem like a house instead of a room, it fools no one. I still think of it as prison if you can't get out.'

'OK Lizzie, wait until you see her then tell me what she should be allowed to do, right?'

Entering the room, Faith called across in what Lizzie considered to be an outdoor-pitch voice.

'Hi Mum, Granny. Look who's here?'

Lizzie pushed forward, squeezing past Faith, who was taking up most of the doorway. Her vision swam as she saw the tiny body of her grandmother perched like a china doll in a single bed. She looked hardly bigger than a seven year old, dressed, as usual, in a freshly laundered nightdress with a lacy collar.

'Granny, how lovely to see you. Oh Granny, you gave me a nightie just like that years ago, do you remember? You said it was like something a bride would wear and you gave it to me. Did brides wear winceyette with little blue flowers and pearly buttons right up to the neck in your day?'

Lizzie sat down beside her grandmother and stroked the scant grey hair which barely covered the old woman's skull. Taking one of her grandmother's dry, cold hands in her own, she kissed her gently on the cheek and the powdery, papery skin sank beneath her lips. 'Oh, I've missed you Granny.'

'Good to see you Lizzie, I hoped you'd manage to take some time off for us.'

'Hi Mum, sorry. I haven't realised how much I wanted to be with Granny until just now. But you know I'll always come if you want me. Is she OK?'

'I'm here Lizzie, I can answer for myself now.' Her grandmother's voice was clear and precise, stronger than she'd expected.

'I want to ask you something, girl. You'll hardly remember your great-grandmother, my mother, Cathy. But I have to trust someone to take on her story. There's a mystery around her. I was never quite sure where she fitted in to her family. I know she was the youngest but there was something else she always held back on, never let me get close. She'd change the subject once I started asking about them all. Do you remember her at all, my love?'

Lizzie's mother, Annie, moved across the room to the other side of the bed, stroking her mother's free hand, which was lying like an injured bird on the snowy counterpane.

'I do, Mum,' Annie replied, cutting across the conversation. 'I remember she had a soft Cork brogue, which would waft across the room like a bygone memory or the scent of a summer passed. I loved my grandmother so very much and we've all always wondered why she never went back to her home near Derryleague, or anywhere else in Ireland for that matter, since she left as a teenager.'

Lizzie had so often heard about the mystery surrounding her great-grandmother's departure from her home in West Cork that she didn't pay much attention, letting her gaze wander over the characterless room.

'I want to die knowing Lizzie will take this on, Annie; she's the detective in our family, the one with the great contacts, and she knows everyone.'

A snort from Faith was muffled by a cough, before she interrupted.

'Lizzie's the one to do it alright, Gran.' Faith's face was beaming now, both dimples showing, enjoying the scene before her. 'She was tellin' me on the way here how she has the great TV contacts an' all. I'm just a teacher, with a degree in history from Queens University. But sure she's definitely the one to do the searching alright.'

Lizzie was cornered. "Game, set and match to Faith," she

thought. "Well anyway, what could be the harm in doing a bit of internet searching and making a few phone calls?"

'I've a bundle of letters in my locker here, came from my cousin,' her grandmother pressed on. 'We wrote to each other for years and she knew all about the family. She's written here about Cathy, my mother, the one I want to know more about. I've kept them for you, Lizzie. Annie, can you...'

Lizzie watched her mother bend down and rifle through the locker beside the bed. It wasn't a utilitarian metal cabinet, like the hospital ones, but it still offended Lizzie's sense of style. A basic mass-produced item deceiving no one with its cladding of cheap wood veneer. Lizzie wondered whether that summed up the place – false letterboxes, artificial door knockers and cheap furnishings. She frowned, hoping the caring was real.

'Here, I think this might be what Mum's looking for.'

Annie leaned on the side of the mattress and levered herself upright before handing the pack of letters across the bed, bypassing the old woman and presenting them with a flourish to Lizzie.

Lizzie's grandmother sighed, resting back on her pillows. 'That's the one, Annie. A bunch of letters from my cousins in Derryleague. They still live near where she grew up. Now I need a sleep. Come and see me tomorrow Lizzie, and we'll talk more about it. About what I know, and what you need to find out.'

'We'll go now girls, leave her sleep awhile. I'll just let the carers know we're away.'

'An' I need the loo, Granny, so I'll say bye for now,' Faith said. 'See you outside, Lizzie. Take your time, you know what Mum's like, she'll find a carer then want to know all about them. She's away now but we're far from away ourselves. Pinot Gringo? Please...'

'Well Granny, as usual that was a whistle-stop visit. Can I do anything for you? Pillows, drink of water?'

28

'Lizzie, I'm exhausted. So glad you are here. Just promise me one thing girl, don't let my mother's memory be disgraced, whatever you find, promise me?'

'Granny, no. No fear of that, I love you, you loved her and I'm sure she loved you back. We'll keep it in the family, whatever it is.'

Slipping her hand behind the fragile neck of her grandmother, she plumped the pillows. A wash of sadness flowed through her as she lowered the old woman's head. Why, she wondered, did it always have to be about family secrets never being told? She knew her great-grandmother had been born around 1900, knew where she had grown up and didn't think she would be difficult to trace. Tucking the letters into her handbag, she tiptoed out of the room, careful not to rattle the false letterbox as she closed the door.

In the early hours of the morning a phone call came, shattering the sleeping house. The night supervisor from Roebank Nursing Home was sorry to inform the family that Mrs Maureen McCormick had died in her sleep.

Chapter 3

Hannah. West Cork: July 1900.

Hannah inched the door closed, fearing she might tangle the jumble of facts in her head by any sudden movement. A new piece of information. It could be useful or dangerous, or at least work to her advantage. This one glittered. A prize to shore up her future. She didn't like Ellen Clancey and she wasn't interested in whether Ellen liked her or not. Not important, not a factor in her life. And her life needed its factors to work for her.

Hannah Daley remembered the cold home of her childess aunt where she'd been raised. There had been too many children and not enough space in Hannah's parents' home and she'd been parcelled out. Still in baby petticoats, she was sent to her mother's sister and there she stayed throughout her childhood. Eventually, the aunt, believing herself to be in poor health, decided that the scant welcome she had been obliged to give her niece had worn out.

By then Hannah had reached the acceptable age, ten years old, and she was marketed as a useful scullery maid. The live-in position in Lahana House had given her a chance to make a life for herself.

During the following decade, she learned to grasp every chance she'd come across to promote herself, whether through favours, secrets or flattery. She knew she could take some advantage from Ellen's situation but needed time to work that out.

Once dismissed by Lady Berish, she made her way along the flagged hallway to the dining room. There she continued setting the silver and dining ware in preparation for the evening meal.

Half an hour later her mistress entered the room, her cheeks bearing a sunset streak of crimson which contrasted with her narrow, blue-white lips. Altogether her face resembled a gathering twilight and her whole demeanour brought to mind an air of chill. When her husband and son followed, by contrast they seemed relaxed. Young Tom caught Hannah's eye and winked.

She knew they usually took a glass or two of something before dinner. It would be a sherry for Lady Berish and the men she thought probably helped themselves to the whiskey. As none of it involved the servants being present she couldn't be sure. She decided the best chance she had of gleaning more information was to maximise her time with the family over the evening meal.

She left the dining room, giving a slight curtsy, a knee bending action which suggested a reluctant bob, and took the stairs two at a time. Reaching her shared attic bedroom, she grabbed her serving cap and clean apron from the top of the child sized dresser jammed between twin beds. Kneeling on the counterpane, she checked her reflection in the rust speckled mirror. It offered a smudged reflection, hooked on a chain between the window and the washstand. Hannah wiped her pale face with a cloth and rubbed the back of her finger against her teeth. Having already caught Tom's eye she wanted to be sure to snare him tonight.

When she returned, the dining room was emitting an unsettling silence. Her early years made her good at detecting pending anger and this one felt about to burst. A threatening thunderstorm weighted the conversation and Landlord Berish said an unusually brief grace. From her standpoint behind his son, she noticed the older man's hand clenched into a tight fist. She stood for a moment enjoying the scent which rose from Tom's body: warm leather, tobacco and horses.

When she leaned over the master, to ladle out the soup, a wash of alcohol and sweat rose to meet her. That was unexpected, it should have been horses. She surmised that he must have come home in his carriage, and the son returned on his own. More news. Lady Berish had said they were out hunting together. Another one for her secrets compartment.

Hannah's nose also told her that neither of the men had returned home in time to wash, although they had changed their shirts. She wondered why Lady Berish bothered with her extensive toilette and reckoned it was highly unlikely that the men noticed.

Catlike, she stalked around the ornate table. She was good at watching and listening and servants were considered invisible. She'd continue watching and listening in the servants' basement kitchen. She was like a prospector, panning the nuggets, giving small low value offerings back to the gossip store. She'd keep those she estimated would have potential value for herself. Hannah smiled as she mulled over the information overheard between Lady Berish and Ellen, knowing that was going to be a valuable treasure.

Looking at her mistress' face, with her high prominent cheekbones and sharp beaky nose pointed down towards tight narrow lips, Hannah thought how unattractive she was although she was considered to be elegant. Hannah supposed that pearls, silk and a complicated hairstyle might persuade her appearance towards some glamour.

But that was quite a different glamour from what was considered attractive around her own home area. Those girls were fair, soft and the colour of hay ripe for harvesting; the type she'd be herself if she'd been half fed she reckoned. The others, dark and glistening, with thick curls and deep eyes, were only slightly less admired. Ellen was one of those. If the dark girls had dimples and generous busts, mothers sought them out for their farmer sons. Either way, everyone agreed that beautiful women should look healthy, ripe, like good fruit, suggesting that plucking would be fun. Lady Berish's features didn't suggest, to Hannah, that she would encourage any plucking.

'How did the proposition go at Ballinvarrig?' the mistress asked, avoiding her husband's eye, and looking speculatively into the oxtail soup. Her words sounded steady and controlled, without any shadow of emotion.

'The Linehans are willing to have us over in the autumn. They suggested the hunt ball.'

'And you, Tom? Will you go to the hunt ball?'

'Aye, Mother, whatever you say.'

'Don't use that language at this table, Tom. "Aye" is peasant speak. "Yes Mother" will do nicely.'

'Yes Mother, I'll go to the hunt ball, and I'll court Miss Linehan and I'll do what you demand that I should do and I'll be stuck with her for as long as need be. Just leave me a bit of peace and a bit of freedom.'

'That's no way to speak to your mother, Tom,' his father muttered. 'And let me tell you there will be no allowance made for your gambling or anything else until we have sorted out this Linehan affair.'

'I'll speak to you later son, after dinner,' Lady Berish announced. 'Thomas, you have some business to do? Or maybe as it's a pleasant evening you will take your evening walk around the grounds.' She paused for a beat.

'Be vigilant now; there's a lot of unrest, uneasiness. I've heard the Land League are becoming fractious again between Derryleague and Dunmanway.'

Hannah removed the bowls before Michael brought around the pheasant and the vegetables. She was unsurprised by the instruction from Lady Berish. When she'd first started working at Lahana it had taken her aback. Her uncle wouldn't have taken instruction from her aunt, she was sure he wouldn't. No other woman she had ever known could tell a man what to do. But Lady Berish could, there was a power within her. Rose and Hannah had often wondered what hold she had over them. Hannah thought it related to money but she'd never shared that with Rose.

It was her intention to stay around after dinner, in the hope of hearing what Lady Berish and Tom would discuss, but her interest was flagging. The conversation was confined to irrelevancies, stilted and without enthusiasm.

'Hannah, bring the tea into the parlour will you, and bring Tom a glass of port when you come,' her mistress commanded.

Stumbling down to the kitchen, bringing the kettle back to the boil on the range top and completing the tea tray inevitably took a few minutes. She refused Michael's offer of help. She didn't need Ellen's brother to hear any revealing information. She was breathless by the time she arrived back upstairs, pushing open the parlour door with her hip, not having a free hand to knock. It was a habit she'd always found useful.

Lady Berish was sitting upright on a maroon velvet chair. It looked uncomfortable but Hannah knew she used that position when the topic under discussion was a challenge.

Tom was leaning rather close and too carelessly to the gable end of the fireplace, arms crossed, with a deep furrow breaking across his usually carefree face.

Hannah set the tray down on one of the many small tables littering the room, taking her time filling the port glass from the decanter on the drinks stand under the window. She carried it on a small silver tray to the table nearest her mistress. As she glanced over at Tom, who would be forced to cross the room to reach his drink, she saw him nod an acknowledgment to her.

'Come and sit Tom, let's finish this in a civilised manner. Right Hannah, that will be all.'

Hannah nodded, bobbed her knee and left the room, failing to fully close the door.

Pushing her shoes off toe to heel, she picked them up. Then, with a tired sigh, she leaned against the wall near the cracked open door, keeping an eye down the corridor in the direction she expected Lord Berish would appear.

'… not going to let this get out, not even to your father.' She heard the older woman's measured tones and slightly raised voice.

'Nothin' to do wit' me, Ma, you must know that.'

'I would like to Tom, except it's not the first time and I can't think why else the girl would come to our door like that. Quite brazen, she was. Quite sure of her facts. She'd only have to go to their parish priest and he start to ask questions. We can't afford it Tom, not now negotiations are at such a critical stage.'

'Suppose I did? "Like her" a bit? What can I do about it now?'

'Nothing. You do nothing. Just stay out of her way. I'll deal with it tomorrow. But I'll be dipping into the funds Father left me. The ones I use to bail you out, and that will be the last. Do you understand me? This alliance with the Linehans, it's the chance of a lifetime. Don't wrinkle your nose at me like that. I know you don't particularly care for her, but it's a big house, a big heritage and we need the security. I pay for everything in this house now; you and your father, you both have to toe the line. Understood?'

'Understood. Thank you, me darling Mama. Always so understanding. Say nothing to Pa?'

'Not this time. Last time he nearly disowned you and what good would that do any of us? But be sure I'm reaching the end of my patience with you. We need you off and married, soon.'

'Well yes, sure, Ma. But I'm going out for some fresh air now. No tables I promise, just a walk.'

Hearing movement, Hannah backed away, attempting to hide in the shadow. As Tom opened the door, a beam of light fell across her skirt and, catching a glimpse, he turned towards her.

Hannah knew he strutted around the females in the house like a young cockerel trying out his charms. It was clear where his appetites led him and the women were flattered as they fluttered around him. She had been surprised by the recent conversations about Ellen, whom she considered naive to have allowed a flirt to go so far. "I've no misunderstanding about Tom myself," she thought. "Sure I've been taken advantage of and used all my life, I know exactly what he is doing."

'Hannah,' he murmured in a husky tone, which suggested tonight he would play less of the cockerel and more of the fox, 'you cheeky monkey. Were you listening to dear Mama and her naughty boy?'

'No Master Tom, I was just fixing my shoe.'

'Ah Hannah, let me see, come on down a bit, away from the door, maybe into the linen press here?'

'No Tom, not tonight,' a smile barely glimmering across her pale thin face. 'I've to see to the kitchen and Mrs Casey will be waiting to go home.'

Running his hand up her leg, he leaned into her; she could feel him harden against her and noticed how his breath quickened. She didn't move away, but relaxed her thigh against him. "What easy prey he is," she thought. "What an eejit to think I am the plaything."

Aloud she murmured, 'I'll be in the orchard tomorrow afternoon, Tom, I've something to do down by the summerhouse. You could maybe help me "fix my shoe" then?'

Chapter 4

Ellen. West Cork: July 1900.

Ellen dragged her feet along the road to Lahana House, basket of clean laundry balanced on her hip. Her head hung low, as it might do if she were protecting herself from a dawn drizzle, but the day was bright and dry.

An early breeze was causing the skirts to flap and drag against her legs; her muscles stretched, relishing the uphill walk. She noticed her breath coming in short rapid bursts. She wasn't sure whether this was due to the stress and sleeplessness of the night before or the "something else" she preferred not to mention.

She'd stood firm against her father when she'd arrived home without Patrick; stalling, begging for one more day. Promising there would be a plan.

'Plan?' her father had yelled, his grey face tinged purple at the edges. 'Plan? there's no plan girl, except you're a disgrace. He'll have to marry ye. No question, but he has nothin', no farm or land to his name. An' until it's settled you'll stay indoors once ye' begin to show. Have ye confessed? Father Tomelty will have to hear it.'

A room full of tension, anxiety helping it rise like one of their mother's loaves, made the arguing continue long into evening. When her brothers and sisters were told, at supper time, only Jimmy held her gaze, his pale eyes bewildered but his head nodding in support. The others looked away and either continued eating or busied themselves clearing and clattering dishes.

Eventually her father agreed to one more day. She'd won that battle but she spent a fidgety night, snatching an hour or two of sleep in the big bed alongside Nora and Mary Anne, her stiff, silent and wide awake sisters. She could feel the hot potato of resentment steaming above them.

Arriving at Lahana, she pushed open the back door with her hip, leaving the clean clothes for Rosie or Hannah to sort though and return.

Settling down at the long kitchen bench, she helped herself to some cold mutton and leftover breakfast bread, eating quickly, choking on the dry texture of stale bread. She was reaching for a tumbler of water when Hannah, fresh in morning uniform, appeared, her nostrils flared, eyebrows raised, flushed with importance.

'Her Ladyship will see you now. Straight away, Ellie, I'm to bring you to her front parlour. You better swally that mouthful, she'll think yer even more of a peasant than ye really are.'

'Her Ladyship will see you now,' mocked Michael, who had just entered the kitchen, moving over to his sister's side. 'Her Ladyship will see you now, indeed! And just who do you think you are, Hannah? We've never spoke like that in here.'

'It's fine Michael, really, leave her. I was expecting a call.'

Tipping the contents of the water tumbler into her mouth, gulping, she spluttered before wiping her face with the back of her hand.

'I don't need you to bring me Hannah, I'm fine on my own thank you.'

Ellen took the stairs two at a time, hoping to put some distance between herself and the maid. She could hear the sharp tap tap of Hannah's boots hurrying to catch up on the stairs behind.

After the exertion of walking uphill and the stress of anticipation, the prickle of sweat dampening her armpits as she knocked the door wasn't a surprise. Pressing her arms to her sides, she hoped it wouldn't show.

Lady Berish was standing by a small table, her back to the window, her silhouette dominating the room. She spoke quietly with a voice filled with ice.

'Good morning, Helen. I've considered what you told me last evening and I have a very generous settlement for you, but first I must ask you to sign this.'

Ellen walked towards the mistress, each step across the wide room felt like a step away from safety. The highly polished wood surface seemed to mock her own unpolished appearance and her boots felt clumsy and unworthy where they met the floor.

She noticed the table contained a white paper and a pile of bank notes. Lady Berish's face was in shadow and there was no indication of whether the table top contents were what required signing.

'I can read and write, Milady,' Ellen's voice quivered as she came towards the table, 'but I need to take my time.'

'You will take up no more of my time, Helen Clancey. I'll read it out to you then you sign it.'

Not indicating that Ellen should either sit or move closer, a thick sheet of paper was lifted from the table by a thin, white hand. Ellen noticed there were no calluses on the fingers and her eye was drawn to the emerald ring, penny sized, sitting proud above the knuckle, as the icy voice began to read.

"I, Helen Clancey, in exchange for the sum of forty pounds sterling will leave Lahana House today, 7th August 1900, never to return. I solemnly swear never to speak of the affair which brought me to Lady Berish's notice.

If I break this assurance, I understand that my family, the Clanceys of Derreena, will be charged with illicit procurement of the aforementioned money. They will be expected to repay in full and with interest immediately or face imprisonment. In addition, the lease on their farm will be cancelled."

'And you will sign it here Helen, now.'

39

'Milady, my name is Ellen, not Helen. Does that matter at all?' Ellen's mouth was dry, speaking was becoming difficult and her heart was jumping all around her ribs, making her feel sick and dizzy.

'Not to me and not to the law. Helen is an English version and this is an English legal document. Here is a pen, I assume you can use a pen? Or you can put your cross here.'

'Thank you Milady, I'm well used to the pen.'

Her shaking hands grasped the stiff page from Lady Berish's outstretched fingers. She heard a loose branch knocking against the windowpane; the wind must have got up she thought, that is why it's knocking. She was distracted by the sound and didn't hear the rest of Lady Berish's directive.

'...suggest America.'

Knock, knock, the glass in the windowpane rattled, the shiny wooden floor seemed unsteady beneath her boots and, embarrassed, she knew her sweat was drying. She had smelt it on herself when she stretched out her arm to take the paper.

Looking up, bewildered by the unfamiliar request, she noticed her mistress sniff. Ellen blushed, humiliated. She was poorly dressed and scarcely groomed, before a woman who, she was sure, would never let herself smell of stale sweat.

She shook her head and grasped at an emergent small shred of confidence, realising the danger she was in.

'Do I keep a copy of this, ma'am, as well as yourself? I'd be feared some might believe I'd stole the money, maybe sometime in the future..' Her resolve was melting before this iceberg of power. 'Like if something might happen to change your mind Milady, would anyone believe my story of how I got the money?'

She heard Lady Berish sigh, a frustrated end-of-tether kind of sigh, and held her breath.

'Really girl, you are most irritating. And no, this is the only copy. You are tiresome indeed. Return to your chores, speak to no one and I will send for you later.'

'Yes ma'am, thank you.'

'Meanwhile I'll craft an affidavit and sign it myself. You can carry it with you to prove the money is rightfully yours. I will, of course, retain this original copy with the conditions. And until and unless you sign this the matter goes nowhere. Do you understand? No money, no agreement, nothing.'

Ellen handed the unsigned document back to the mistress. Her heart had leapt when she'd seen the sum. Forty pounds. Such a fortune, so much more than she had hoped for. But she reckoned that holding out for a copy was the only way she would ever feel safe with such a hoard. She wondered what an affidavit was but expected it was the best she was going to get.

'Thank you, Milady. May I go now?'

'Yes, leave, girl.' Avril Berish had already turned away and was looking out of the window. The branch was knocking harder against the glass and the wind was strengthening, promising a blustery afternoon ahead.

Chapter 5

Hannah. West Cork: July 1900.

Hannah leaned her body as close to the doorframe as she could manage, straining her ears, trying to hear every word. A knot of jealousy formed deep inside as the implication of what she had witnessed hit her like a cold stone in her belly. 'God, I hope she takes the deal,' she muttered. 'I can do plenty with that if she does. I'll not be lettin' on to the others, she'll answer to me.'

Later she watched Lady Berish and Tom eating luncheon in silence as she served, discreetly, not wanting to engage. Tom had widened his hawk yellow eyes in a silent ask. She'd responded with a nod and the shadow of a smile, one which her own eyes didn't answer.

By mid-afternoon she'd escaped the kitchen. She climbed the narrow stairs to the room she shared with Rose and changed out of the dull brown uniform into a summer gown. Slipping the calf length lilac linen shift over her thin shoulders, she watched it encase her slim hips, skimming her knees. She knew it was impractical on a stormy day but she'd rescued it from a heap of cast offs. Lady Berish provided a regular collection for the Skibbereen Poor Law Union. And besides, this was Hannah's only dress. Beguiling was a word she had heard someone use once, and she'd liked the sound of it.

'Hannah girl, you are about to beguile. But sure I can't have old Rose comin' in while I'm sortin' mesel out, can I now?' She pushed a chair against the door and reached under the bed. She'd gathered a clutch of sphagnum moss early that morning. It was soft and green, not like the dry crisp lichen which crept over the stone walls around the house. The moss had been soaking in a bowl of rainwater water and now Hannah squeezed the soft spongy clot to drain out most of the moisture. She wrinkled her nose as the brown tangy bog water drizzled out. She squatted on the floor and pushed it into herself. The bulk felt uncomfortable so far inside. It was further in than she'd ever managed before, and she wondered whether she'd be able to walk.

'Ellie, ye stupid eejit,' she muttered, squeezing her thighs together. 'Do ye know nothing? I could've told ye, but I'm not sure even now d'ye know what caused it, girl?'

She edged down the stairs as specks of moss soaked water dribbled along the inside of her legs. Her only option, to be sure not to be seen from the house, was to cut into the field leading to the summerhouse.

Once she reached the orchard she kept close to the crusty old apple trees, whose trunks were frilled with ivy. No one tended the orchard anymore. It only bore small wizened fruit. That made her feel safe. Some locals would harvest the apples for their own use, but always after dark. The Berishes wouldn't give anything away. The wind was still rising, swooping the grass into a patchwork of shades from dun to green, damaged by lack of rain.

As she neared the summerhouse, she smirked, thinking the name pretentious. Hannah reckoned it was only a notch-up on a greenhouse. Looking across the orchard, she felt her mood droop, seeped in disappointment. She hadn't been there all year and neglect, aided by short summers and long winters, had ruined any grand aspirations the name might have conjured. 'This estate is going downhill,' she muttered. 'I'll be lookin' for another placement soon enough. Get this deal settled first then see what I can get to keep me goin'.'

'Aha. Caught you talkin' ter yersel' there, Hannah. Didn't know I was watchin', did ye?'

'Tom, sometimes you sound more Irish than we do. Yer Ma will knock that out, I'm tellen you.'

'An I'll knock some Irish out of you too, my lovely girleen. Come on in here a minute 'til we get a cuddle.'

'Colleen is the word yer lookin' Tom, not girleen. Ye big dope.'

He pushed open the summerhouse door, putting one hand on its wobbling frame as Hannah stood in the doorway sniffing the damp air. Spores of green algae were creeping up from the lower to the upper panes and mixed with dirt they diminished whatever light struggled through the tightly closed windows. The wind was locked outside and the summerhouse air inside was heavy and humid, like a long closed church.

Hannah lowered her head and twisted a clutch of lilac linen between her fingers, feigning reluctance to step inside. Tom's broad hand on the small of her back nudged her forward.

'Give me a kiss then, Hannah. Tell me I'm lookin' gorgeous today. I've given up a visit to the tables for this.'

Hannah lifted her head as he pushed her through the doorway; she stopped to let her body fall back, smiling as she felt him strain against the soft deerskin of his breeches. He leaned into her and she heard, once again, the quickening breath as his hand ran up her leg. She knew he'd soon be feeling the scratchy curly cluster of hair which shielded her as he tried to prise her thighs apart with his long smooth fingers.

She put her hand over his, stopping any further probing. 'Over here Tom, it's more comfortable.'

'Over here,' she repeated. His eyes widened with surprise as he looked at her hand pulling his out from under her skirt.

'There's somewhere here we can be together.'

"So, here's meself," she thought. "Lying on a heap of old sacks, insides stuffed with bog moss and yer man only interested in his own pleasure. I need to make sure I get a reward for this."

Aloud she murmured, stroking his back, 'Well, let's take our time Tom. There's no one going to see us here now is there?'

Lying back, she stretched her legs apart and watched as he pulled the fabric of her shift up to her waist. He smiled, his hawk eyes sparkling, as he saw she wasn't wearing any drawers. He dipped his head to nuzzle between her legs.

'No, Tom. Kiss me, come up here. I don't want that.'

She could smell Tom's breath now hot and heavy, a mix of onions and meat. He tugged at his breeches and gave a sigh as he was released. Lowering himself into her he closed his eyes, missing the flash of pain which crossed her face with every thrust, pushing the moss further inside.

'Wow, Hannah, you are some beauty,' he muttered as he sank his weight on top of her.

'I am so.' She agreed, twirling a lock of his damp hair around her finger.

'Will we do this again, Hannah darlin'? You know how to look after a man so you do.'

'Maybe next week,' Hannah offered, smiling up at him, trying to breathe under him, knowing she had caught her prey.

Tom pulled himself up, giving her a brief kiss on the cheek while he refastened the front of his breeches. He left the summerhouse swaggering and whistling. Looking at him walking confidently between the trees, she was satisfied. His carelessness suited her purpose very well.

Once he was out of sight, Hannah squatted over the sack for some minutes, extracting the moss, wincing where she was tender and trying to brush the sackcloth markings and watery stains off her linen dress.

Chapter 6

Ellen. West Cork: July 1900.

'Forty pounds. Forty whole pounds. A fortune. Three or near four years pay at least. Money upfront.' Ellen's mind buzzed. 'I've a plan and I'll stick to it. This child will have a name and I won't go begging, that's for sure. God almighty, I hope I wasn't too forward with the Berish woman, but I couldn't take the risk now, could I?'

She worked through the usual chores, clearing up in the kitchen, feeding the hens and gathering the eggs. Once that was done she climbed the stairs and checked outside the bedroom doors for laundry. She called in with the housekeeper to ask were there any repairs to be taken down to her brothers. She loitered in the kitchen, listening with feigned interest to the most trivial domestic gossip. The minutes stretched, no word came from the mistress and she dawdled when it was time to leave.

Gathering the soiled laundry into her basket, she pulled her apron over her head and set it on the kitchen bench, ready for the morning. After a moment she changed her mind, dropping it in the basket, she might be expected to wash and return it in the morning.

Ellen inched away from the house. She had to persuade her feet to keep moving while her stomach was trying to overcome the churning, which was threatening to create an explosion.

'Perhaps I was mistaken, maybe asking for this affiwhatsit was a step too far for her ladyship.'

The wind had dropped and the calm silence of the evening supplied a morsel of comfort. Ellen looked around at the familiar surroundings as though for the first time and wondered in what way her world was about to change. She set her basket down on a perch of stones, the memory of an old wall, and leaned alongside.

Looking across at the gnarled apple trees, blossoms long gone, fruit small, holding little promise of anything other than crab apple, she wondered, 'Is it like that with humans too? I need to know. How long will it be before the baby comes? What will I need to do to keep myself safe?'

Ellen's hand moved to stroke her belly and let her mind drift, imagining how it would be, the feeling of swelling over many months. She thought about the outcome of a careful harvest. The result was ripe juicy fruit, not dried out little crab apples. She knew damaged fruit was the result of neglect.

She drew a breath and asked the heavens, 'What should I do to make this child a good ripe fruit? And how long will it be before I bear it?'

'What's that, Ellie? Talkin' ter yersel' now?'

'Hannah, what's the matter? Your good outfit all crumpled. I'm just sitting waiting. I was expecting a message from the mistress, but maybe it'll come tomorrow.'

'What message, Ellie? Ye can tell me, girl. I'm your friend.'

'No Hannah, I'm not to speak of it. It's between me and the mistress. Where have you been anyway? Your lovely dress,' Ellen giggled. 'It's all wet and you're waddling like a duck.'

'Mind yer own business, Ellie. You've troubles enough.'

'What do you know of my troubles, Hannah? You been snoopin' at doors again?'

A familiar voice called across to the girls, cutting into the antipathy thickening between them. It was Michael. 'Sissie, can ye come on in the house now. Mistress is lookin' for ye.'

The command made her both shudder and tense. Torn

between being glad to bring the wondering to an end and wishing she could be somewhere else. She slipped off the stone, leaving the basket of washing on the ground. In a few seconds she reached the house where her brother was beckoning her in by the back door.

She glanced a farewell over her shoulder, in time to see the sly smile on Hannah's face. She had kicked the washing basket over and scuffed the garments, watching them soak up surplus damp from the soft spongy soil.

Ellen didn't stop, her rosy face became flushed and sweating in her hurry. She could feel her plait coming loose and thick dark curls clinging to the back of her neck. Checking right and left, she stumbled to the top of the stairs, wanting to avoid Tom. She hoped this meeting would be brief and unobserved.

'Please God. Please God. Let her give me the money. I'll go away so I will. She'll never see or hear from me again. Promise.'

'What's that Sissie?' Michael's words came as a surprise, his breath hot at her ear. 'What's going on? Is it to do with the child? I saw Patrick today but I didn't say anything. He was down at the stables workin'. The poor man. What've ye done to him, Sis? He has nothing, you know that. Nothin' more than an agricultural labourer, to be hired out wherever he can find work. An' these grand people won't care about has he a child to feed.'

'I'm sorting it out, Michael. Don't worry. I have it under control. Now I need to see Lady Berish, so on ye go. I'll tell it all later. And please Michael, say nothing about it at home.'

Ellen was surprised by the confident sound her knocking made on the parlour door. Echoing around the stairs, it seemed to bounce off the stone lintels and linger until the faintest resonance dissolved into the hallway's chamber.

'Come,' Lady Berish's clipped tone, commanding and unwelcoming, penetrated the door. "That is her world, confident and secure within," thought Ellen. "It is a different world to without. I am certainly the one who is without but maybe it's possible I can turn that."

Entering the parlour was almost familiar. This time she didn't gape at the elaborate decorations and superfluous items scattered across the surfaces. She knew where the furniture was positioned and wasn't distracted by wondering why anyone might need four small tables in one room. And that fireplace, so big, but only for comfort, no cooking irons. She was not in awe, she almost felt pity for the family. Nothing domestic was being created here; it was part of a world designed for formality.

'This is getting tiresome, Helen. And I don't have any more time to waste. Lean on this table, take the quill pen, I've already dipped it, and sign your statement. And yes, indeed,' she sighed, as though bored with a conversation which hadn't started.

Ellen had stepped forward, her question pre-empted, lodged on the roof of her mouth.

'Before you ask again, I have the affidavit here, my sworn word. So you won't be accused of theft but equally I don't expect a word to be breathed outside this room. Ever. Understood?'

'Yes, Lady Berish. Understood.'

Ellen's legs wobbled as she walked towards the dipped pen Lady Berish was holding out disdainfully, as though it were soiled. She manoeuvred herself past the ornate armchair to the table in front of the fireplace with its weak, new lit flickers of flame.

Bending over she read the lines with care, running her finger beneath each line to make sure she understood. Then she set the pen nib, her hand directing it exactly where she needed the ink to meet the stiff pale paper and signed her name at the bottom of the page. Ellen Clancey of Derreena.

'And here is your affidavit and payment. I don't want to see you back at this house again, ever. Never contact any of us again. You can leave behind whatever possessions of this house you take care of. And now go away. Understood?'

'Yes, Milady.' Ellen took the document and the bank notes. She thought it would probably be the last time she'd see the grandmother of her child. Although she didn't expect the slightest flicker of any emotion, she had to look up to confirm. The woman's stone blue eyes reminded her of a blackbird's egg. Her senses told her that there was an injustice being done, particularly to her child, but she didn't have time to reason why that would be.

Tucking the precious papers in her skirt pocket, she left the room, without any acknowledgment, or suggestion of gratitude. She had got what she came for and wanted to be far away from Lady Berish and her cold eyes.

Once outside the house, the stifling tension and the stress of waiting which had threatened to overwhelm her earlier eased. She leaned against the gate at the foot of the drive, taking deep breaths. She hoped that might calm her heart, which was galloping across her chest, feeling as if it might jump out. Shaking her head she realised that now she could be a mother. She had money, choices. She was no longer a servant.

Arriving where she'd left the laundry basket she sighed at the mess Hannah had made. Then, having packed the clothes away, Ellen left the heaped basket just inside the gate on the sweeping gravel driveway. She reckoned that whoever would find it and take care of it was no longer her concern. Straightening her back, she walked down the valley towards the Riley family croft.

Chapter 7

Ellen. West Cork: July 1900.

The day soothed into evening as the light began to leave the sky and Ellen's mood responded, her thoughts and plans settling down as she clarified her next move.

The past couple of days had been tough, but now she believed there might be some control over her future. 'As long as Patrick goes with the plan, I'll be fine,' she muttered. 'Independent. And my child will have a name.' Her whole being felt lighter than it had last evening, when her mother had untied the bodice.

Walking at a gentle pace down the valley, she let her hand brush against the hedgerows, decorated with heavy-lidded purple fuchsia and bright orange, tiny-petalled mombresia. Ellen realised it was not the first time she'd thought about the contrast between outward appearance and inward suffering.

Beauty was certainly all around, as was the poverty and exhaustion being lived inside the crofts. She knew many families were subsisting rather than thriving. Remembering her schooldays, she'd seen plenty of examples of hardship: hungry children, clothed in scruffy leftovers, who shivered all winter. She'd taken it for granted, the cold, the malnutrition and the range of childhood illnesses. Many came to early deaths. Plenty of people were short of what was needed. There was no food for children at midday and, when there was any offer of casual work, they wouldn't be at school at all.

Reluctant to go too close to the Riley croft, Ellen waited

by the small copse on the mound above their dwelling. She was clearly visible, standing in front of the trees. She knew it wouldn't take long before someone, probably one of Patrick's brothers, told him she was there. Since Easter when they first began dancing together at the cross-roads she'd heard them sniggering. And when she was seen with him, it created a rumour that they were courting.

The figure of a short muscular man emerged from the croft, climbing the slope towards her. She smiled and waved as he approached. He had something of a swagger to his gait, which she liked. There was an atmosphere of defiance around him, and maybe a bit of fun.

Over the months of their friendship, or was it ever more than that, she wondered, Ellen had come to understand Patrick's personality. She knew an oblique approach always got better results from him than a straightforward request. She'd heard his brothers say he was cussed, awkward, contrary. But his limited chances, his lack of schooling and of any encouragement, had left him frustrated and poor. Well, she reckoned, she might be about to change that.

'Hey Pat, come on over here.' She lifted both arms up now, waving, making sure he knew she was happy and keen. She wanted to put him at his ease before any discussion began.

Patrick stepped up his stride, keeping his hands in the pockets of his mud-caked breeches, which were straining at his hips. Ellen thought they had probably belonged to his father, a slightly built man, bred from hungry parents. His waistcoat distracted from the breeches, defiant red and brown tweed, poached from the donations basket at Lahana. He always wore the same waistcoat, with a short-sleeved shirt and flat cap, it was the farm labourer's expected dress. The men usually shrugged off extra clothing when they started to work, stripping down to bare chest in summer months. Although it was practical it was also something the girls admired.

As he came closer she could see the stubble on his face and remembered he'd only shave on a Saturday night, to be ready for Sunday Mass. The beginnings of a beard glinted now and then, catching the setting sun.

'Great ter see ye' Ellie. What's the craic?'

'Come on over here and tell me, Patrick, have ye time to be over to our house the night?'

'I have so. What would be keepin' me?'

'Ah do you not have much keeping ye these days, Pat? Is there no chance of anythin' changing around here?'

'I'm stuck here as a farm labourer as well ye know, Ellie girl. Why're ye askin'? Have ye heard of an opportunity for me or what?'

'Nothing so grand I'm afraid boy, though it would be good if I could help. I would so, you know that.'

'Aye, I do, Ellie. Your Michael did well to get himself a butler job at the big house. But I'm ground down, so I am. Been wonderin' whether I'd maybe take my chance in Bantry town or Skibbereen. Might there be an opening there, do ye think? Away from this tied farm business altogether.'

'An' sure what would you be doin' in Skibbereen or Bantry, Pat? Is there any opportunity you've seen?'

'Not yet, Ellie, but they are takin' on at the gasworks station in Skibbereen. Coal up from Baltimore in the lighters an' men needed to carry, an' so on. I've a day off comin' up next week an' I'm going into town.'

'An' yer Mam, Pat. What's she sayin'?'

'Difficult alright Ellie, she needs the money comin' in. I'd have to get good work.'

'I've a mind to go to Bantry or Skibbereen too, Pat. Or further maybe. I've a bit of a problem about stayin' here at the minute, and the big house has just let me go. The job's gone, so it is.'

'Ellie, I can't take ye with me, you know that. How'd it

look? An' what's your trouble anyway? Ye didn't want to lose that grand job; it was steady money, so it was.'

'Ach maybe. Five shilling a week, sixty hours' work in the house an' the laundry to do at home.'

'Well, sure that's a pound a month Ellie, twelve pound a year. If ye had that twelve pound all at once ye could set yersel' up.'

'Wouldn't that be great, Pat? Twelve pounds all in a lump sum. What would you do with that, if ye had it?'

'I'll never see it, Ellie. Sure, the tightest farmer around here would be pushed to save a couple of pounds in a year so he would.'

'Well just supposin', Pat, just think on it.'

'I'd set up in a rented room in Bantry an' look for work, but 'til I found work I could feed mesel' for a while. I'd do that so I would. Maybe get work drivin' a cart or as a builder's labourer. Or cyclin', making deliveries like. Better than stuck here forever. There's no room for me to turn around in there.' Patrick jerked his head in the direction of the croft. Ellen, letting him lead the conversation to a place which suited her, nodded agreement. She put her arm across his back, squeezing his shoulder, needing him to remember they had, occasionally, been seen as a couple.

'I'm in trouble, Pat, and I need someone to help me out. Maybe there's a chance I could help you out in return?'

Widening his eyes, raising his eyebrows to disappear under his cap, and dropping his jaw a fraction, Patrick displayed rarely seen emotion.

'Now I've a conversation to have. Serious like.'

'Will we walk, Ellie? I'm gettin' cold standing here.'

The spongy ground made a comfortable carpet. Ellen, barefoot, felt the soft mosses sponging between her toes and concentrated on pushing her feet as far down as she could, a distraction from what was to come. Her full skirt lapped over the bulge in its pocket where the notes lay. She wondered whether she should have kept the apron, which might have helped conceal the money. Wrapping her shawl around her shoulders, she tried again.

'So Pat, I'm in a bit of a bad way. I'm having a child, not sure when exactly, but I think it will come before Christmas.'

'Get away! I don't believe it. Are ye sure?'

Patrick stopped walking and looked at Ellen in horror. His eyes never leaving hers, she thought he was scared of what he might see if he dropped them.

'Ye're ruined so ye are. I'd never have thought that of ye, Ellie. Whose is it at all?'

'Well now Pat, that's the favour I'm askin'. See they think, you an' me like, we're courting. So they do.'

Ellen burned. She put the back of her hand against her cheek and felt the heat on her cool knuckles. She wasn't sure she could go on. Shame and embarrassment combined to bring a hot splash from her neck to her forehead and her throat constricted.

'What're ye sayin', girl. Sure, I've never touched ye. A bit of a court, well sure, and a walk home after the dancing. An' I mind thon night when we stopped a while and felt like doin' a bit more. But we didn't. I'm not that kind of fella. An' I thought ye weren't that kind of woman. Yer disgraced, Ellie.'

'Patrick. Ten pounds. I've ten pounds from the father to keep for myself. But I've never to say his name. Never go near him again. An' if you'll let me name you, take me with you to Bantry, or further if ye want, I've ten pounds for us. Could ye think on it Pat, please.'

They walked up the hill and then, facing the stone wall bounding a field full of Berish's cattle, Patrick sank his elbows onto its uneven surface. Ellen held her breath. He hadn't said anything and she wondered whether she should increase the offer. She had four times that amount but knew she'd need the money and didn't want to lose control over her future.

'Please, Patrick. Here is how I see it. You an' me, we say the child is ours and we go to Bantry, get away from the families, less disgrace. We'll go as man and wife, no one knows us in the town. Set up together. I'll look after the place, get the food an' everything, maybe even take in laundry or do a bit of sewing. You could get some good work.' Ellen couldn't look at Patrick while the words tumbled out, fixing her eyes on the cows, wishing she had a fraction of their untroubled approach to life.

'Then,' she swallowed, determined to finish. 'Well then, once the babby is born, if you don't want to continue, then I'll come home an' you can go your own way. But it'll give you a start, Pat. You'll never get away from here if you don't go now.'

'I'm to come to your house tonight, am I? An' your father will be minded to give me a thrashing, and I never even got the pleasure of ye?'

'Well, yes. That was my plan. But maybe forget it. I should just go home an' say I don't know the father an' they will all wonder anyway was it yourself. I've never been seen with anyone else. But I won't say who, I won't land you in it. I'll just stay at home disgraced, shunned, ashamed. An' my child will have no name.'

The wind lifted, a gust blew across Patrick's face and Ellen saw him hesitate as he realised she was right. With her own money, he knew she would stand alone and face the scandal, but there would always be a doubt cast on him.

'Patrick I'm gettin' cold now too, the evening's drawin' in and I have to be home. Are you with me or no. It's your call.'

'I will do the honourable thing so I will. There's no real choice now, is there? If I don't the whole country will think it's me anyway and my family will be shamed. But one thing is certain, if I agree we have to stick to the plan. I'm not marryin' ye, Ellie. Once the babby is born ye come back here an' I get on wi' my life in Bantry, Skibbereen or maybe it will be Cork. The best offer I can get. An' no more said about it. But I will give my name, no child should come into the world without a name.'

Ellen linked his arm into hers, it was the start of a business arrangement which would look like intimacy. Resigned as well as relieved, she gave a low, slow sigh, as they turned to face the direction of the Clancey farm.

Chapter 8

Lizzie & Rufus. Bristol: August 2022.

Leaves were crisping in Bristol, not yet turning, and summer was still keeping its door ajar for late sunshine. Maureen McCormick had been buried for three months and the promise Lizzie had made her grandmother had not been forgotten.

'I'm happy wherever we go kid, as long as I can be a creative.' Rufus' head was bent over his camera, not looking up as he fiddled with the viewfinder. 'This camera of mine is amazing, super-wide angle and telephoto lens, so I'll go anywhere snappy happy.'

'Yup, West Cork is reputedly very snappy happy, Rufie, you should be OK there.'

'An' what about a bit of down-time with Lizzie too?'

'OK. So it's a visit to my great-grandmother's home and lovely snappy places on the way?'

'Yup, Irish pubs, stunning scenery and everyone happy, no?'

They left their Bristol flat, their eyes scratching with the early wakening, and tumbled into Lizzie's car. The city birds were just beginning to chat and hop on the scrappy dry trees lining the road in front of their flat.

'It's a bum-numbingly long drive across Wales to catch the midday sailing to Rosslare, Rufie. Please, settle back and don't annoy me with any smart-aleck remarks about "are we nearly there?"'

Rufus's childish singsong response of 'I can see the sea' raised the shadow of a smile from Lizzie as she watched him kick off his shoes, push back his seat and wrap himself into his new, top of the range sleeping bag.

Lizzie's dimple cracked her cheek as a wash of holiday freedom trilled through her fingers, tapping on the steering wheel. Negotiating the empty city streets, following signs for M4 West, gave the journey a sense of adventure.

Several hours and country music albums later, the horizon turned blue and flat. Lizzie nudged the sleeping Rufus.

'Glittering sea, baby boy. Wanna take a photie?'

Rufus's eyes, reluctant to be brought to attention, were rubbed by the back of his hand, encouraging them to focus.

'We are well used to glittering seas, Lizzie.' He mumbled through a yawn. 'No need to sound so surprised. We had plenty during the past long hot summer, weekends with our Devon maties.'

'I know, it's gorgeous there, but when I see a sea I'm going to travel across I feel excited, like I'm going on holiday.'

'Actually, you are, Liz.' Rufus smiled as he squeezed her knee, just below the ragged edge of her denim shorts.

'Don't do that while I'm driving Rufie, too distracting.'

'Just a bit higher, don't be such a prude, you used to be such fun. You'd have had me pulling over by now!'

'Nope. And I never would have, but we can stop for a break if you want, we've loads of time.'

'Just look at those mountains Liz, all purple, grey and dusky brown. See how they complement that sharp metallic light? I can't wait to get out with the camera. Yeah, let's pull over for a minute, the clouds might change and then the whole picture will be different.'

Lizzie was glad of a chance to stop. Sensing excitement in Rufus's voice, she knew how much he had been looking forward to spending time behind his lens. She'd promised him plenty of coastal scenery, keeping him happy while family history was being unearthed.

Leaning against the warm car body, she stretched her limbs back into shape as Rufus squatted by the grassy verge. He was clicking and turning his camera at different angles while Lizzie squinted at the mountains. She wondered why those same colours on a curtain would scream at each other in discomfort, whilst on a hillside they gently blended. Thoughts of curtains and back home were pushed aside. Now she was here, in the moment, it was her "going on a bear hunt" mission. Not being entirely sure what the nature of the bear itself would turn out to be.

'I'm really excited, Rufus, about this holiday. I'll be honouring Granny's wish, making contact with distant cousins in West Cork, and then the Ring of Kerry.'

'Ah, the famous Ring of Kerry.' Looking up at her, Rufus angled his camera so as to catch her profile. 'Full of American tourists, d'ye reckon, Liz?'

'Bristol ones, more like! Big photography country though. All waiting to be captured, just waiting for you, Rufus.'

'Did you say you'd been before?'

'A couple of times, Faith, Mum and I. We went but I don't remember too much about it. Just the Cork voices. Granny talked like that a bit too. I know you think I'm silly, but there is an unreachable part of my life, one I just can't put my finger on.'

'I could reach it for you Liz, just tell me where?'

'God, you're impossible. No soul. What if I said I need to fill the gap, complete the tale, stroke the back and pet the shoulder? Or, to put it another way, if I said there was a little missing, unreachable part of me, what would you say?'

'Bonkers.'

'C'mon, get into the car, Rufus, there's no sense in you today. And pull that ponytail tighter, its drifting down your neck, like a boozy floozy!'

'Holidays, kiddo, holidays. Relaxed attire.'

It was midday when they arrived in the busy car dock

at Fishguard harbour. The sun seemed to be searching for unprotected bare skin, burning Lizzie's shoulders. Her head was protected beneath the narrow brim of her raffia sunhat but she wriggled her hips, tugging at the hem of her shorts.

'Stand right behind me, Rufus,' she pleaded. 'I need to wriggle and scratch. Hope no one is looking.'

'I'll take advantage of that request, Liz.' Rufus pushed closer. 'I'll give you a wriggle and a scratch myself. We didn't book a cabin, did we?'

While Rufus wriggled his fingers between her buttocks, Lizzie's attention wandered. She heard many accents seeping into the atmosphere, it seemed an unmarked border had been crossed. A babel mix of Irish, German and indefinable other tones — mumbled, relaxed, indecipherable — maybe, she wondered, was the sun over the yardarm somewhere?

Leaning back against Rufus, she began to relax after the long drive and her ears sought out the lilting Cork voices amongst the waiting passengers. Vaguely familiar and comforting, maybe they were the sounds of her great-grandmother, Cathy. Her mystery woman.

Although Rufus and Lizzie were early, they were never going to be first in the queue. The hot car grumbled as it crawled onto the ferry, reminding them both that this was a far longer journey than its usual route from Bristol flat to stables.

After some stair climbing and drifting about on the third deck they chose a lime coloured plastic padded couch by a window. With water bottles and paperbacks in hand they settled back, watching the curtain coloured coastline drift out of sight.

After a few hours, calm sea gave way to a choppy harbour. Gulls calling outside their windows told them they had arrived in Ireland.

'Car drivers return to car deck and wait in their cars.' An overhead announcement pealed through the passenger deck. 'Foot passengers remain on board until advised to leave,'

'Let's go kiddo, I'll drive. Safer that way.'

'That's us in the republic now, Rufus. I'm so excited. Can't wait to see it all, and you're gonna love it.'

Lizzie yawned, the long day was far from over. With the gangway lowered, cars rumbled down in a nose to tail queue, leaving the small harbour behind within minutes. Speeding out of town, with afternoon sun glinting off the Wexford hills, the curving empty roads offered frequent appearances of pubs and whitewashed cottages.

'I thought these were only set up for the tourists. I hope it hasn't gone too diddly dee?'

'What's diddly dee Liz? Anything to do with this agricultural machinery blocking my view?'

'Watch it, he's turning right, don't expect him to tell you though. And, well diddly dee, it's like we all speak the same language but somehow the words mean different things. So, see that tatty billboard over the hedge there? You wouldn't say "Up the lads" along an English hedge because you'd know people would have no idea who the lads were or even where up is.'

'Ha, gotcha. Here are "Dungarvan, the home of Panadol," now that's enough to give anyone a headache!'

'I think you're getting the idea now Rufie, we'll be stopping in about half an hour, a wee place called Kilmeaden.'

The sun had disappeared by the time they arrived at the top end of a small village. They slowed down, hearing the satnav declare "You have reached your destination". A tired sigh escaped Rufus. Lizzie craned her neck, looking down the wide empty street edged by small cottages and new-build bungalows. Black, white and ochre colours vied for attention. The main central character, O'Donnell's Public House, had been decorated to look like a traditional thatched cottage.

'Here we are mister Englishman, our first pit stop. All window boxed up and welcoming Failte signs over the door.'

'Now that is diddly dee,' Rufus muttered as he pulled cautiously into the vacant car park, trying to decide which of the identical empty spaces would suit him best. 'The front looks all Disney and here at the back it's beer crates and tractor parts.'

They stepped inside the pub, which was no longer Disney. Flags hug from the beams and posters, old photographs and replica guns, commemorating the Irish Revolution, decorated the walls. The bar displayed a gleaming array of drinks on tap.

Within minutes they'd been noticed, greeted 'How ye doin'?' and shown upstairs to a bedroom with a view of the back yard. Lizzie went straight down to the bar, while Rufus stayed by the door, peering cautiously at the menu pinned to the brown painted wood panel at its back.

In the bar room, Lizzie was the only female. Two men in green overalls, their high-vis yellow jackets slouched across chair backs, occupied all the space in front of the polished wooden counter-top. At their feet lay a morose collie dog. Her attempt to catch the barman's eye failed. He appeared to be busy, shining the badges on the pumps. After a few minutes, Rufus came to her side to see whether she wanted to eat, which triggered a response from the barman.

His deferential 'What can I get you sir?' sent a shudder through Lizzie, and, ignoring Rufus, she responded, 'One Carlsburg, one Guinness please.'

'What in God's name would it have been like trying to get a drink in here a hundred years ago?' Lizzie licked the back of her hand, the lager had spilled when she took a sip.

Rufus laughed. 'I don't think you would have been let in the door, never mind been allowed to buy the drinks!'

Rufus, looking at her over the rim of his Guinness, saw her mouth scrunched up like a disappointed child. 'Now sit down and behave,' he chuckled. 'I'm going to take a closer look at these Irish heroes; want to know a bit about West Cork.

Meeting your cousins tomorrow after all, an' I need to seem a bit savvy.'

'Seeing these flags there's not much doubt about where we are, Rufie. Look at those tricolours draped like bunting across every door frame. And the harps. And shamrocks everywhere. We could be stepping back in time too, except for that enormous TV on the wall and the wifi code on the beermats. I'll just log on while you update yourself and then maybe we can eat?'

She always needed wifi, reckoning it was part of her job. Her day-to-day working life, uncovering details of celebrities, tales of woe, anything which might make an interesting story for the magazine. It needed to be fed fresh morsels on a regular basis. But engaging with a parallel universe to her own much more modest lifestyle didn't make her unhappy. Many of her friends' priorities had changed since the coronavirus pandemic, and hers had too.

"I've never given much value to stories of celebrities and glamour." The thought made her smile, recalling occasions when she'd wound Faith up with a bit of sisterly bragging. She had sometimes been invited, briefly, into the lives of the rich or famous. Mostly her work entailed a visit to a nearby town where politicians were creating a rumpus or where a sea wall had burst, endangering lives. Sometimes, even with the mundane, she felt out of her depth, paddling below the plimsoll line, never letting on how she was struggling.

Lizzie decided she wouldn't work today, but she scrolled through her online account using the O'Donnell's broadband, clicking "like", adding an occasional emoji. She always kept up with her friends, Facebook or otherwise.

'Listen to this, Lizzie. Three hundred women took part in The Easter Rising. Here's a copy of the declaration itself, a diddly dee I suppose you would say. Yeah well, touristy souvenir sort of thing, can be purchased from the bar for ten euro. Might get us one tomorrow after breakfast, what d'you think? It's fascinating stuff. Nineteen sixteen must have been one hell of a year.'

'Strong women were treated equally then, were they, Rufie? Maybe I should have looked a bit more military at the bar just now!'

'OK Liz, off the high horse, let's eat. I'm thinking Irish stew and soda bread, what about you?'

'Quinois, butternut squash and red pepper please, with a side salad.'

'No one would ever accuse you of blending in, Liz. You just take your trendy I-am-a-journalist-from-the-big-city attitude with you wherever you go!'

'That's simply not fair Rufus, you know I'm not someone with an attitude, I just know what I like. Now get that order in before I have to send for the authorities!'

Chapter 9

Lizzie & Rufus. West Cork: August 2022.

The following morning the sound of cattle and the cranking of tractors woke them at sunrise. 'Full Irish?' they were asked at breakfast, their host not expecting the response to be other than an enthusiastic affirmative. The generous platefuls were taken in the bar room where they had spent the previous evening. Having packed and paid they were out in the car park by nine o'clock.

'You drive, Liz? Careful mind, these roads are narrow and you don't know what's round the corner.'

'Yeah, yeah, I'll do that, and I've never known what's round the corner, actually. Put some music on, will you?'

Rufus pushed buttons and fiddled with knobs until some classical music drifted into the car. He kept one hand on the camera slung around his neck, not paying much attention to which station he selected.

'What's this relative exactly, Liz?'

'Well, let's see, Granny's mother Cathy was this man Danny's great aunt. Anyway I think so.'

'Not too close then?'

'Well, no, but the promise I made to Granny about unravelling this mystery has to start somewhere. Don't you think if anyone should be able to shed light on it, he should?'

'And are there others?'

'Well, those letters Granny gave me were full of this one and that one. They were written by this man's mother. So I thought that he would be my best bet.'

'This scenery is amazing,' Rufus interrupted, keener on the landscape than on Lizzie's pursuit. 'It's like a picture postcard of old Ireland. All those tiny cottages. The tumbledown ones are best. Did people really live in them?'

'Yup, they did. And sometimes you'll see new builds alongside, on the same plot. It's as though the family is saying, "Look, we are still here. Still part of the same story, just with the en-suite, the internet an' all." I love it, that feeling of continuity.'

'Hmm. Not my thing really, but whatever you say. Let's stop a minute. I'd like to capture this. An old shack in a stony field, with the sheep wandering through.'

Lizzie sat in the car, the soft morning air breezing through the open window as she watched Rufus crouching and snapping and angling like a spider. Her eyes travelled over his spare frame, with the memory of his sharp hipbones against hers. She giggled softly, running her fingers through her hair. It had been a challenge alright, the creaky mattress in Kilmeaden.

'How do you do it?' she murmured. 'Everyone I know works out or starves to look like you, and you don't. It seems to come so easy.' The bare flesh of Rufus' legs protruded above the ankle of his fashionably tight jeans which in turn enhanced the outline of his neat, bony hips. She loved his style. Once she'd told her sister, 'He's so smart. Angular from the front, and long haired hippy from the back.'

If asked, she might admit to loving his independence and his ability to distance himself when it suited him. His photography she considered a marvel.

Lizzie had teased him about it once, soon after they'd met. 'I'd only ever think of using my phone to take photographs, and you are the only person I know uses a camera.'

Now she waved her hand through the window. 'And when you've finished today, will you be able to download and then will I have a record of our trip? Saves me keepin' track.'

'All done now Liz, you can head off again, me duck.'

It was another hour before they reached the town sign for Derryleague, "Doire Dhá Liag." 'I'm lovin' these Gaelic signs, the heritage and identity...' Lizzie started to say.

'OK, hold the sentiment please,' Rufus interrupted. 'Wanna pull over, comb hair, do lippy? I'm going for a quick pee.'

Lizzie, checking her hair and makeup in the car mirror, wondered whether she'd been wrong to impose herself on scarcely known relatives. She peered closely at the mirror, checking her teeth. She couldn't arrive at the door with the remnants of breakfast still visible. Nodding approval at the bright yellow and navy scarf, she was pleased to see it offset her short denim dress. The sun was encouraging a hint of freckles, giving her face a milky coffee tint and she approved of that too. Finally she twisted her thick dark hair into a casual ponytail.

'I'm good to go.' Her eyes glistened, amber as setting toffee. 'Hurry up Rufie, we don't want to be late, they might be waiting.'

A short drive outside the village of Derryleague brought them to the front of a well-kept modern bungalow, surrounded by sloping fields.

'No old cabin ruin here,' remarked Rufus, as Lizzie switched off the engine and took a few deep breaths. She was surprised to find that suddenly her palms were sweating and her heart was racing.

The front door opened before they were out of the car. 'Come in come in, we've been looking forward to seein' ye.' She knew her cousin's wife was nearly the same age as Annie, her mother, but this sandy haired woman had the face of someone younger.

'You must be Lizzie. I'm Marie, Danny's wife. In here so, he'll be just delighted to see you.'

Marie stood back, stretching out her arm inviting them to walk past, through the brightly wallpapered hallway into a large, wide windowed room.

Danny was seated at the table and rose to shake her hand firmly, using both of his, for a fraction longer than she expected. Lizzie felt a jolt of something. Was it familiarity she wondered? His deep Clancey colouring, certainly, she'd almost expected that. But the proportions of his face, the distance between nose tip and chin and the full straight eyebrows. He reminded her of one of the uncles she'd known as a child. She relaxed, feeling that he was someone she would describe as "genuine," someone she could trust. She smiled, she'd been right to come. Once her hand had been released, a younger man, dressed in slim fitting corduroy jeans and a designer hooded sweatshirt, rose to greet them.

'This is Paul, he's your cousin from Galway, well, third or fourth cousin anyway. He was passing through, and we asked him to stay a while to meet ye.'

While Paul and Rufus shook hands, sizing each other up, Lizzie looked around, recognising this room as the centre of a long established home. The walls were hung with family photographs, alongside certificates testifying achievements from school to university. On one wall a red light flickered beneath the image of the Sacred Heart, followed by John F. Kennedy and then a Pope.

There was a range in one corner and an electric cooker in the other. Heavier saucepans and dishes appeared to occupy most surfaces but a set of elegant fine china stacked on the worktop suggested guests were expected. Lizzie felt a longing to be part of this network, and optimistic about the visit.

A long kitchen table stood beneath the front window. It had been laid over with a roll of wallpaper, its back covered with lines, names, dates and crossings out, all annotated in different colours. Danny and Paul invited Lizzie over with a wave whilst Marie made tea. Rufus found a chair near the door, telling them he'd like to admire the view.

Lizzie leaned right across the table as soon as she spotted

the name Catherine Clancey. 'Catherine, that's my Cathy!' she exclaimed, delighted to find her great-grandmother's detail so soon. 'But who is this someone called George? Both he and Cathy are recorded as the children of Ellen.' Lizzie shook her head, as the newcomer to the party, she knew she should hold back and she hoped her enthusiasm hadn't seemed rude.

'I'm sure that's wrong! We need to change that. Look.' She pressed her hand down onto the line on the paper as though to embed her truth into the family tree.

'That's Cathy, my great-granny. Well she was Ellen's sister, so she needs to be moved to the line above. No idea who George is though.'

Lizzie was handed a cup of tea and a plate of cake, while Paul and Danny asked for her own family tree. She tried her best, but she hadn't really been prepared for this so most of the record was from memory. The wallpaper soon became peppered, "populated" Paul called it; he was a teacher and seemed to know what he was doing, with family names, relationships and significant dates.

The chart of a third tree was brought to the table. It was an older version, and she watched as the family trees became a copse, with straggling branches; she searched for connecting pathways between them.

"I can enjoy this now", she thought. Excitement and familiarity made her feel more connected to this mystery quest than she had expected. She glanced over at Rufus from time to time, hoping he wasn't getting bored.

All four ran eager fingers over the treasures. The connections between names were sometimes familiar, others newly uncovered, while they got to know each other over tea, served in Marie's best china.

Rufus was sipping his tea. He seemed intent on ignoring the growing copse of family trees, which were threatening to reach plantation size indoors.

He listened for a while, as they recounted names and details, then called across the room. 'All these family members. They are descending like friendly, chatty ghosts, I'd have liked to photograph them.'

No one answered. Draining his cup, he brushed cakecrumbs off his tee shirt, stretched and wandered outside.

'I'm glad she's having a good time,' he mumbled, checking the view through the lens of his camera. 'She knows I don't like excitement and speculation, usually more than content with my own company. I'll stay on the edge if you don't mind.'

After a few minutes it sounded like there was a change of plan. 'Hey, come with us, Rufie, we're going to visit Joe. He's ninety. He's the one who lives all alone now on what was great-granny's original family home.'

Rufus sighed, enthusiasm wasn't his style. 'I'll drive then.' He waved the car keys, retrieved from Lizzie on arrival, up into the air, no one could mistake his intention.

The car edged and cruised down a couple of miles of uneven roads, slowing as the route contracted away from the village. On either side, heavy hedgerows were laden with late summer wildflowers, their vibrant clashing of orange, blue, yellow and purple brightening the route.

'Watch now Rufus, it's just around this bend.' Danny, sitting in the front seat, gave Rufus only a second's notice before directing him to turn into a narrow lane, an unmade track with a line of grass running down the centre.

Bumping and jolting, they came to a stop at an informal opening, the relic of a front farmyard. Lizzie tumbled out the back of the car. Her attention was caught by a single storey whitewashed wreck of a farmhouse standing to one side of the yard. There were worn cobbles showing through the grass and weeds which looked well established. The half rotten front door, showing the remnants of red paint, was ajar. It suggested a welcome to any small scuttling creatures who might be looking for a home.

Marie, Danny and Paul disappeared into the twentieth century farmhouse to the left, where Joe lived. Lizzie stood for a moment in the warm sunshine, smelling the hay and a soft sweet mixture of old farm dust and honeysuckle.

'Aren't you going in, Liz? Everyone is waiting for you.'

'Rufus, how must it have been for my great-grandmother, living in this remote, beautiful place with her brothers and sisters?' Lizzie shook her head; she'd taken off her scarf and her hair felt heavy in the heat.

'Granny often told me Cathy used to run home from school, without shoes, over these fields. They are beautiful fields but surely too rough for a child's small foot.'

'Don't know about rough, but think they were tough in those days. I'll stay out here for a bit now, you go on in.'

Lizzie turned from the warm scented air and meandered through a rusting iron gate. There had been gravel laid on the path once, now it was just visible through the green. Stepping into the house, she blinked as her eyes adjusted to the shade inside.

Danny and Marie had arranged chairs, with a spare one for her, so they could face Joe whilst asking questions. Paul was looking in a drawer which was half hidden by a heap of newspapers. Lizzie was introduced, loudly, several times to the upright figure, dressed in a tweed jacket and a sweater which looked hand knitted and new. She had the impression that he was smartly dressed for the visit and wondered how he would have been given notice. She bent towards him as his 'Good ter see ye' greeting was followed by a handshake. Her hand was damp with a mixture of anxiety and sweat, his felt confidently firm and powdery dry.

'Aye, that's James,' in response to a dog-eared photograph of a stern-looking man. 'He married a German woman, in America.' 'No, that's my mother, Deirdre. She was a Regan, not one of the Clancey sisters.' A faded Mass card was held before him. 'Ah, that's the good-looking one. Nora, she died young.' Danny had found some newspaper cuttings in an overflowing drawer, triggering a fine spray of dust and dry smell of must to rise.

'Skibbereen Eagle, 1910. What's this about, Joe?'

''Twas a case around these parts, long time ago. Farmer's daughter, near Enniskean, servant in another farmer's house. Her father brought the case for getting his daughter in a bad way.'

'Goodness, Danny, five hundred pounds it says here. Would that be right? An awful lot of money I'd have thought. Seduction, that is what they are calling it, happened in 1904 by my reading. Took the family a while to bring it to court then.'

'Well, it was a disgrace and the farmer would expect money to keep the child. And no one would marry his daughter, of course, so he had to keep her as well.'

'Would that be usual, Joe?' Lizzie's interest was piqued. This was a story she'd enjoy writing up as a journalist. And the timing, not too far from the time Cathy was born, gave it some relevance to her own search.

Danny smiled at her, handing her the flimsy yellowed cutting. 'The big sum is unusual alright, that's probably why Joe kept it. Obtaining money for a wrong-doing isn't.'

'Says here "she was employed quarterly at a wage of ten pounds per annum. And 'the defendant' "sat up late at night with her when the rest were in bed." Hmm. Not much to be guilty of there, I wouldn't say.'

'Not much else, Lizzie?' Marie asked. 'A reputation was a lot in those days.'

'Well also,' Lizzie held the cutting at arm's length, the typeset was cramped and smudged. 'Also, he took her to races and places of amusement. And then relations continued from "the harvest 1905 until spring 1907." She "became a mother" in May that year.'

'Why didn't he marry the girl?' Marie leaned over Lizzie's shoulder, keen to read the details.

'Well, I'm amazed Marie. A relationship between a servant and a rich farmer which lasted several years and sounded like they had a good time together, ends up in court.'

'Gets worse, Lizzie. Read this. "The action brought by the father for damages for the seduction of his daughter." He is described as being "in the capacity of master." Wow. Times have changed.'

'Yup. Cheek of it. Master indeed. No man would be described as my master, that's for sure.'

'Maybe a woman couldn't bring a case, we don't really know, do we, Lizzie? And such a fortune. Five hundred pounds. The equivalent of fifty years of her salary. Can that be right, Joe?'

Joe shook his head, his face betraying no emotion. Lizzie wasn't sure whether he was disapproving or simply not wanting to discuss the details.

'Sure I can't remember all that.' Joe interrupted. He sounded impatient. 'They weren't ours so it's no bother ter me.'

Danny took the newspaper cutting from Lizzie and replaced it in the drawer. 'He kept it, Lizzie. We will probably never know why.'

'I remember your Granny though. Bought me a bugle once for Christmas. Sent it over from London.'

'My Great-Granny, not my Granny.'

Joe's palest of blue eyes were filmed, like damp river-stones. Lizzie had the impression that he would only answer questions if he felt like doing so.

Danny and Paul continued to bring out images of old people, young people, American people, but no glimpse of her great-grandmother could be found. She reckoned there had been more discussion around the woman in the newspaper cutting than there had been about Cathy.

Impatient, and aware that their time with Joe was limited,

74

she pushed into the fast-flowing river of conversation. 'I'd really like to know how many brothers and sisters she had.' Looking up enquiringly at her cousins, seeking approval. Of course they knew him well and she wanted to tread carefully.

'That's Catherine Clancey,' Danny clarified.

'I think they were all born here, in that old house across the yard, every one of them, like me,' Joe said.

'Do you know how many were born there? Great-Granny Cathy and who else?'

'Well there was Ellen, the eldest, then...' He recited a litany of names, none of whom sounded familiar to Lizzie.

'But what about Catherine. Do you know why she left to go to England?' Squeaking her request, Lizzie knew it sounded desperate. 'Her daughter, my own granny, asked me to come here and find out whether there is anyone who might know.'

'Cathy? Well, sure, there's no mystery about it. There just wasn't room for her. My father had married first and brought his wife into the house. Then Dan married and he needed to bring a wife in, an' we had to split the farm. That was in 1916 and so she had to go. It was a grand chance for her, an opportunity to move on in life, live in the city.'

Lizzie did a quick calculation. The girl – great-grandmother – would have been fifteen or sixteen, her year of birth was unclear, but Annie had been sure it was around 1900.

'How frightening, to be leaving this lovely country place where everyone knows everyone else and to have to go away on your own to London, and there was a war on.'

'And,' Danny reminded her, shaking his head, 'there was a revolution going on at home too.'

Joe's shrug suggested these events were only to be expected in life. He didn't seem to tire. Lizzie asked, 'Would he want a cup of tea?' and heard her voice sound hard and scratchy, too high a pitch amid the velvet soft West Cork tones.

Marie frowned, speaking quietly. 'Now, Lizzie, Joe has been

looking after himself here for many years, he wouldn't want ye going into the kitchen.' One glance towards the dim, untidy kitchen convinced her. She shuddered, wondering what might scurry behind the sack of potatoes lying half opened on the floor.

Danny got to his feet again, grimacing as his knees creaked, his large hands picking delicately as a bird through another old box, which stuffed with official looking documents.

Lizzie watched him for a few moments. 'I'll just pop outside then, for a bit of fresh air and see how Rufus is getting on. Won't be long.' She wanted to make the most of the opportunity to look around the farm buildings, hoping to feel the presence of the family in the atmosphere.

Wandering outside, feeling long grass brushing against her bare calves she sensed a church-like calm seeping out from the older buildings.

'I love it here but I am a bit disappointed, Rufus,' she mumbled, rubbing the palm of her hand across the back of his head. 'I'm none the wiser. It's an ordinary family living an ordinary life. We've been discussing some interesting backgrounds but no mystery here.'

Rufus didn't look up, he was crouched behind an old stone wall, angling his lens through a gap. 'The countryside here is untamed, Liz. I could stay here all day.'

'Me too,' whispered Lizzie. 'Me too.'

A figure emerged from the dim interior of the farmhouse, it was Danny. Stepping cautiously over the yard, avoiding the small potholes hidden amongst the stones and weeds, he appeared to be clutching a document. As he approached, he offered it to them.

'Look now at this, Lizzie. Ye'll read something of your great-granny here.'

Taking the paper, she noted the title "Census of Ireland 1901".

Her eyes scanned the brittle yellowed sheet, its creases almost perforating the page. The handwriting was elegant, a flowing script, which looked as though it had been created by a nib pen. 'Oh really, "an enumerator of the baroncy" wrote this. I wonder why they didn't fill it in themselves?'

Rufus came to stand beside her, poising his camera over the document. Lizzie raised her eyebrows at Danny, silently requesting permission. Danny nodded and Rufus clicked.

'Here it says Irish speaking people, cannot read or write.'

'Aye, that'll be cannot read or write English, Lizzie. Irish wasn't an option, not for official records. These are British documents, see?'

'But look here, a list of those present in the house that census night. Some were scholars, so they would read and write, wouldn't they?'

'Yes, but the authorities were very hard on people in those days. Everything had to be done exactly and it would only be the head of the household who would be allowed to complete the form. Or if they couldn't write English then it would be the enumerator.'

'Not the girl scholars then? Even though they were, let's see what. Ellen, she was twenty-seven?'

'Read on, girl.'

Lizzie's eyes scanned the page. The last entry was a Catherine Riley, granddaughter, aged six months.

'But she was Cathy Clancey, not Riley.' She looked up at Danny, her eyes pleading for an explanation.

'I think your great-granny was a baby born into this family. A child of one of their own girls. Which one we wouldn't be sure now, and why they gave her the name of Riley. Maybe they thought the girl would marry the father.'

Lizzie's heart leaped. 'I can't believe I'm holding actual evidence of baby Catherine, baby great-grandma. And she wasn't who they all thought her to be.'

'Mystery solved then, Liz?'

'Just beginning I'd say Rufus.'

Lizzy cradled the census document as she handed it back.

'Never a word of it said in Mum's family, Danny. Maybe no one ever knew?'

Chapter 10

Lizzie & Joe. *West Cork: August 2022.*

Danny and Rufus were getting to know one another, discussing the scenery, the best places for photographs and appeared intent on staying outdoors. Lizzie returned to the dim interior of the farmhouse where Marie was sitting alone with Joe.

'Paul had to leave, the wife collected him, he said to say goodbye.'

'Just us then Joe. You, me and Lizzie here. Cathy's great-granddaughter, remember?'

Joe hadn't moved, not even shifted in his chair. As he looked up, she thought his pale eyes looked less opaque. They seemed to be holding a glimmer, a suggestion, of mischief, brightening his face.

Marie leaned forward, a curtain of shiny fair hair shielding her face.

'Joe, did you ever hear tell of the Riley family? Did they live nearby? D'ye know what ever happened to them now?'

'They lived down near Lahana, ye can visit the old croft. All dead. No children. Nothing left of the Rileys.'

He sighed, seeming resigned at having to confirm that a line of enquiry was now closed.

The sound of a steel band interrupted the silence.

'Oops, sorry Lizzie, Joe, my phone. Have to take this. It's work.'

Lizzie held her breath. She was waiting for the right moment to break the comfortable silence being faintly penetrated by the sound of Marie's voice outside.

'It's amazing, isn't it Joe? This quiet countryside, miles from the nearest town, and it has such a fine mobile phone signal. Sometimes I can't get a signal at all in Bristol.'

Joe sucked in his cheeks, nodding. The wide eyed look he gave her suggested he knew secrets of the mobile phone system which he couldn't divulge.

'Joe, may we just have a chat here until Marie comes back?'

His ninety-year-old eyes glistened, as though this could be something he'd enjoy. Maybe, Lizzie thought, the phone signal wasn't the only thing that was loud and clear in this quiet countryside.

'What do ye really want to know?'

'I want to know about the relationship between Ellen and Catherine. Or do you call her Cathy?'

He chuckled. A moment's silence made Lizzie wonder whether there was going to be a response. Then it came. 'Sure, Ellen was Cathy's mother.'

It was as she'd expected. Not wanting to disappoint him, she tried to look surprised and leaned forward, as she'd watched Marie do, keen to catch every word.

'Did she know?' Lizzie asked, her heart pounding.

Joe gave another chuckle, almost a giggle. 'Of course she knew. We all knew. Did you not know?'

Lizzie's face flushed with embarrassment. She hadn't wanted to mislead him but what she really wanted to know was whether there had been love for the child.

'Had she been taken in reluctantly, or had she been more fully accepted, I wonder?'

'What's that, girl?'

'Did she call her Mammy?'

'No, of course not. Ellen went to America. Came back a couple of times too. Cathy had her grandmother, Mary Clancey here. That was her Mammy.'

'But I think she lived here until she went to London. She was happy?'

'She was just the same as all the others. She was the youngest, they all missed her when she went.'

Marie appeared at the doorway, beckoning. It was time to go. Lizzie said goodbye and, at Marie's sign, kissed him on his papery whiskery cheek. Drained by the emotions which had washed through her, she couldn't tell whether she felt sad or happy.

The afternoon was merging into evening as they drove away. Swallows were swooping low in front of the car and the light was still good, although shadows were beginning to pool and spill across the road.

'Would ye like to visit the old house where the Rileys lived?'

Danny directed Rufus without any suggestion of doing otherwise. It seemed to Lizzie that perhaps this had always been the plan. Within a minute they pulled up in front of a tumbledown stone building, one storey, one room, one window.

Lizzie, Rufus and Danny got out, leaving Marie to make another phone call.

'Clogs to clogs,' Rufus murmured to Lizzie. 'No need to skip a generation here. And where would they have put an extra wife and baby in this tiny dwelling?'

He pointed and clicked while Lizzie went into the remains of the cabin.

'Would they have had land?' she asked, keen to assure herself that the living was not as meagre as the tumbledown patch suggested.

'No land.' Danny shook his head, confident about his facts. Lizzie wondered again whether he had prepared. 'They were tied to the big house down the road here. Even the Clanceys had to give a man and a horse for a day a week. That was a whole day to the landlord, and if you didn't, then they kicked you off the farm.'

'And this Riley family?'

'Worked to the big house, no question at all. Women to the housework, men to the farm. I heard though that Michael Clancey, Joe's father, well he was a butler at the house.'

'So they all knew each other, the youngsters in both families?'

'Sure, and would have danced at the cross-roads platform. That's where ye met your partner in those days.'

'What's that Danny? Did they put up a platform for a festival or what?'

'Well it was a tradition, not now of course. Bit of a structure to dance on at a junction outside most townlands in Ireland. On Sunday afternoons during summertime the youngsters would gather and do a set dance or even a solo if they wanted to show their skills. It was a social thing and it wasn't just the youngsters, anyone with a fiddle would be there.'

'Sounds like fun actually. It wasn't all doom and gloom was it?'

'Liz, lets put it aside now and get some dinner. Danny is there somewhere we can take you and Marie for the evening?'

The following morning they rose late. Marie and Danny had both gone to work, leaving a generous supply of wheaten bread and cereal. Lizzie made them cups of tea in the empty kitchen which they drank standing up looking out over the fields.

'I really like this Liz, it's all here, the colours, the light on the fields, the shape of the trees against the sky. No traffic either, or any noise at all really.'

'Will we go into Skibbereen today, Rufie? I'd like to visit the Heritage Centre. Want to see if we can find the 1911 census. Tell us whether Catherine Riley lived out there on the family farm during her young days. She might have gone with her mother to live in the tiny cabin, with her father's family. Or even, did she go to America for a few years?'

The drive from Derryleague to the Heritage Centre in Skibbereen took them through rolling hills, winding roads and 'Look, on the horizon, there's Bantry Bay. Can we stop?'

'On the way back, Liz. We need to get on, it's still a half hour drive to Skibbereen.'

The Heritage Centre was easy to find, bordered on one side by the Ilen river and just off the main street. Its car park was empty as they pulled in.

The grey stone walls of the centre, which they'd been told by Danny was an old gasworks building, were lightened by large glass windows. This made it less forbidding than the grey stones suggested and, basking in midmorning sunshine, it gave an appearance of welcome. Tiny speckles of light were glittering on the surface of the river and the entire area looked holiday-ready. The West Cork Hotel, across the street, caught Lizzie's attention.

'I'm nervous, Rufie, I don't know what we might find, and I didn't take much breakfast. Can we go over for a coffee first?'

'No Liz, we can't. No delay now. Let's get on with this then we can start off to the Ring of Kerry tomorrow. Otherwise you'll dilly dally around here for days, and that wasn't the deal.'

'I know, you're right, let's go. Coffee after. Yeah?'

Pushing the heavy door open, they paused at the entrance. The meagre light inside was unexpected, although there were illuminated posters depicting desperately thin figures on display all around the walls.

'It's appropriate, isn't it?' Lizzie whispered, with church like reverence, 'to see the place dim and solemn. We are looking at a history of Irish emigration, famine and general poverty-related loss after all.'

The tall man at reception seemed to reflect the solemnity of the room. He wore his shirt buttoned up with a striped tie sitting neatly beneath his collar. Lizzie hadn't seen Rufus wearing a tie since her grandmother's funeral. Her throat constricted at the memory.

She approached the counter, having been told by Marie that this was a drop-in centre and they wouldn't need an appointment.

'Sorry, ma'am, the genealogist isn't back until Thursday. I can't help you now, she's the one you need to speak to.'

Lizzie's eyes filled with tears, and she bit her lip, swallowing hard. She decided she wasn't going to beg or look needy. Not in front of this serious stranger.

'See, sir.' Rufus stepped in, noticing Lizzie's distress, 'We have to leave tomorrow, and we've come over from England especially to find out what we can.' Rufus leaned an elbow on the highly polished mahogany counter, taking care to pull his lanky frame back. He didn't want to appear threatening.

'We have it here, the photograph of the document. See on my mobile screen. I can email it to you. Shall I?'

'I'll take a look for ye so I will, but I don't recognise that address.'

'Maybe even a Clancey or a Riley?'

'Lizzie, why don't you take a look around the exhibition while Mr err Robert, yes, thank you, Robert, does a bit of a search for us?'

Disappointed, she took Rufus's advice and crossed the dim hall to view the exhibition. She felt steeped in sadness; her own concerns a mere flicker amid this great tragedy. There was extreme and unremitting misery of the story being relived around the exhibition walls. Death, numbers, data, all piled on top of one another and she didn't know what it meant.

She read that the Great Famine of 1856 caused the death of a million people out of a population of eight and a half million. That was staggering. The Covid pandemic had caused the deaths of less than two hundred thousand in Britain, out of a population of sixty six and a half million. Her head swirled. The proportion of death in famine was enormous compared to the pandemic, and she understood that the pandemic caused more deaths than anyone expected. She couldn't do the maths, hadn't much grasp on the numbers, but she could see it was awful.

Then she read about the complexity between the policies, the absentee landlords and the ill feeling amongst landlords and tenant farmers. It looked as though few of the farmers were really tenants, more like labourers or slaves and, absorbed by the illustrations, she hoped her ancestors weren't depicted.

Of course, she reasoned, there were many survivors. The Clanceys were solid farmers, albeit indentured as Danny had described, but how about the Rileys? What would their ancestors have suffered, and what remnants of that absolute poverty would have been evident less than fifty years later when Cathy had been born?

She felt a surge of patriotism, and a sense of injustice, for people and circumstances she'd never known.

"Which of the children survived?" she wondered. "The youngest or the oldest? Was there any similarity to the way we behaved in the Covid pandemic? People would have been grasping at straws of hope, anywhere there might be a glimmer, a relaxing of occurrences. No," she shook her head to clear the thought from her mind, "of course it wasn't like the pandemic, we had enough. I shouldn't even compare the two events."

Lizzie remembered the weeks of isolation which had brought her closer to Rufus. They worked from home, walked to shops self-conscious in their steamed up masks and kept to the 'exercise once a day' rule along the empty city streets. They had enough food and enough money and even, unlike so many of their friends, a tiny garden. And then there had been regular news bulletins, not that she had believed them all.

She looked, aghast, at the depictions of a nation starving. She thought it must have been terrifying not to know what was happening in the next county. And no idea when or if it might ever end.

Moving onto the next poster, Lizzie called across the room. 'Food was plentiful, Rufus. Look at this, leaving Ireland in ferry loads, the only food failure was the potato crop. But there had been lots of food, it must have been politics and policy failure.'

As the room was empty apart from herself, Rufus and Robert at the desk, Lizzie continued.

'Surely, had the famine occurred today, it would have been sorted out at government level? Or would it?'

Lizzie walked slowly around the walls, considering the exhibits, unperturbed by Rufus's lack of response.

'I'm wondering now, Rufus, did the potato famine cause long-term poverty? Was the anger and mobilisation of the 1916 Easter Rising a further-down-the-line effect of what had happened fifty years earlier? Was Ireland ever the same again after the famine, and will our world ever be the same again after the pandemic?'

Lizzie shook her head, hoping it might not have been as bad as it looked. 'Let's go, please,' she turned, assuming Rufus would be behind her by now, expecting his discussion with Robert to have concluded. 'I've seen enough sorrow for one day. My heart will break if I learn anymore.'

But he was not behind her; he was still at the desk, across the room. Stretching forward, Rufus was speaking to Robert as they looked at the computer screen. She wandered across to join them, trying to fix her face into a smile.

'I have it now for you. 1901 and another 1911. Here, take a look. You are welcome to keep these.'

Robert handed them two documents. As they had seen before, Catherine Riley, was recorded as being a granddaughter, six months old in 1901. The second document showed Catherine Clancey, daughter, ten years old in 1911.

'So something changed after the 1901 census and made the family accept Catherine, Cathy, my great-granny as their daughter when she was really their granddaughter. What could it have been?'

Robert leaned over the counter, lowering his voice to a respectful, confidential tone.

'They maybe expected the girl to marry and so the child was already named for the father's family. Then she didn't marry, and so they reverted. But they took her in as one of their own, fair play to them. Nothing to be ashamed of there, so there isn't.'

Clutching the printouts and thanking Robert, they left the centre, crossed the car park and walked over the footbridge to the West Cork Hotel.

'Wow, this is lovely,' Lizzie turned to Rufus as they took in the ornate surroundings. 'We can sit near the window, overlooking the river with the swans or grab a seat here in this gorgeous mahogany panelled snug. Coffee and a bite to eat would go down well I reckon.'

'I wonder dare I photograph the view outside, down the river? Not inside, of course not, but it's all very Georgian and elegant isn't it Liz?'

'No diddly dee here, eh?'

'An' I just wanted to say, looking at this second document, Rufus, Ellen is missing.' Rufus was trying to catch the waiter's attention, so she raised her voice. 'Now that I know she was Cathy's mother I need to find her before we can say we understand the full story. Are you up for that?'

'Liz! Shush please. You are drawing attention to yourself. Yes I'm up for it, 'course. Whatever.'

Lizzie leaned back in her chair, a satisfied grin on her face as she reached across the table for the menu.

Chapter 11

Lizzie. Bristol: February 2023.

Lizzie's back throbbed. She stretched, resting her eyes away from the computer screen for a few minutes before resuming the tap tap swipe download. Sorting through facts and contradictions.

She had spent months searching a plethora of family trees, websites promising records which turned out to be unavailable, trails of other Ellen Clanceys; hopes lifted and smashed. The events around her great-great-grandmother weren't yielding information easily but that meant that every clue, however small, was cherished.

'The trail is so faint, Ellen. I never thought much about who you might be until last year. Now you are no longer with us I promise to uncover the truth, so my family will know you.'

Lizzie knew she needed the story, the real human reason, the why. Knowing Ellen's name was absent from the 1911 census and that Cathy's name changed from Riley back to Clancey wasn't enough.

She hadn't shared much of the information with her family until now and decided that a call to her sister was long overdue.

'Hi Faith, how're you doing? Have you got time for a chat?'

Faith was often busy, and even if she wasn't busy, Lizzie would say she wasn't a great one for lengthy phone calls.

'Social diary's as full as ever, Lizzie. Marking papers, preparing lesson plans, agreeing with Mother..'

'There is a real mystery I want your advice on, Faith,' Lizzie interrupted, her voice bright with light-hearted enthusiasm. 'A child whose name is changed from one census to the next, a mother who disappears, and we don't know when, where or why. And they are both related to us, three and four generations back.'

'Well Lizzie, I can see you're off again on one of your notions. I'd say it is unusual alright. But maybe in those days they did things differently. Don't judge what happened then against how things are now. I've kids in my school who are perfectly well-adjusted and well-loved who only have one parent, and in fact several in my school who have same sex parents.'

'Oh, so cool, Faith. Hasn't Norn' Ireland come on!'

'Yup, it would have been unthinkable a century ago, even twenty years ago, Ireland or no Ireland. North or south. And today is a very different culture, much more forward looking and of course, much more affluent than it was in those days. Maybe it wasn't so unusual then or maybe it was terrible.'

There was a pause before Faith continued, becoming more engaged with the conversation, less positive about the advances made by modern Ireland.

'And even today, when you hear about the nuns, the orphanages scandals, and the laundries it sounds horrendous. But really, we've no idea.'

Encouraged by her sister's interest, Lizzie plunged in, attempting to make her findings as intriguing as possible.

'Well, Faith, what I'm seeing is a woman who seems to be dependent on her family to look after her and her child. Then she just disappears. I'd like to hear her side of the story, wouldn't you?'

'Go on, I was in the middle of marking papers but I'm listening now.'

'I've the birth certificate. Her baby was born in Cork but no baptismal certificate, so I don't know how long she was living in the city, forty-five miles away from her home. Shouldn't think she had any money. I wonder could she have been anywhere else holding her own independently?'

'No idea Sis, but I reckon you're about to tell me!'

'I think a workhouse perhaps or maybe she was in an abusive relationship which she had to leave?'

'Maybe. You are certainly asking a lot of questions here. What is it you want me to do about it anyways?'

'That's just it Faith, I've an idea. Why don't you come over here for a few days, get a bit of a break? I've spent months puzzling over a mystery as to what happened to our great-grandmother, and her mother too. It would be lovely to get your take on it. Maybe we could hang out together for a bit, go to the theatre maybe or clubbing?'

'Lizzie, I'm too old for clubbing and we do have theatres in Belfast, Coleraine too as it happens. But I might come over and take a look around Bristol, see what you've been up to. They are my ancestors too.'

'The people I've met so far are really lovely Faith, and the story is just intriguing, so it is. But I need to be careful, I don't want to offend anyone. I'd be glad to talk to you about it.'

'Offend anyone? You? You'll put your two big feet in wherever you can find a wee gap, I've seen that alright.'

Faith couldn't see the reaction this caused as Lizzie's cheeks burned, her eyes swam and she bit her lip. She remembered the many times when she had spoken out of turn to her sister, commenting on her choice of friends or clothes. She'd never meant to, it just came out.

She was great with people at work, and with all those who imagined they were celebrities and glamorous personalities. But when it came to her more intimate circle, she had often been told she went too far.

'Lizzie, you are generous, funny and reliable and most of the time your friends stay loyal.' Her sister's voice broke through her thoughts and she shook her head, concentrating on their here and now conversation.

'Remind me where you've got to then, on this search of yours?'

'Well I did tell you last summer when I met some cousins and the oldest cousin of all.'

'Yes, you did. You do know how to enjoy yourself don't you, Liz?'

'Really, they're great. I feel as though I have expanded the family..'

'And. Get to the point. What's the bottom line so far?'

'Well, Granny's mother was called Catherine Riley at birth, then on the second census she is Catherine Clancey, by that time she is ten years old.'

'OK and her parentage?'

'Bit of a mystery there Faith. Apparently…'

'Apparently? Either it is fact or it isn't a fact. This was a long time ago. Tell me what you know, not what you think might have happened.'

'OK. Yes. It's agreed that Ellen, the eldest daughter in the Clancey family, had a baby called Catherine who was registered as grandchild in the household and her surname was Riley.'

'So far, so good. Get on with it, I'm not exactly riveted.'

'Then, at the next census, you know, when I said she's the daughter, and a Clancey, no Riley about it? Well on that census Ellen, her mum, has gone. Apparently to America.'

'Apparently, Lizzie. Come on. Did she or didn't she?'

'Don't know Faith, Old Joe said she did.'

' Look, all well and good Lizzie, but that was months ago. What've you been doing about it since?'

'Busy with work, bit of online researching, Christmas with Rufus's family. Time just slipped by.' Lizzie took a breath and paused. She was going in for the big ask and felt like she was suggesting a first date.

'You know what I'd really like to do, Faith? With you? Let's have a few days away. Changed my mind suddenly.'

'As you do, Liz.'

'Yeah well. Not Bristol, but New York. How about that for an innovative idea from the big foot?'

'An' when would I get the time to go to New York ? Or the money?'

'Faith, listen. We can go and visit Ellis Island, that's where I think they would have emigrated to. We could see what it was really like and how she got on. Maybe even find out where she went? Did she have any other children? Did she go with the Riley person?'

Lizzie swallowed, she'd been unaware just how much she wanted her sister's company.

'I'll help with your fare.'

'Liz, I'll do you a deal. Find out, Google it or something, there's lots of ways, find out if she was on a passenger list and the date. Then if she was, I tell you, I promise you, we will go together. Easter holidays. How's that sound?'

Lizzie gasped, shocked at her sister's sudden enthusiastic response. Others might not have recognised that response as hugely enthusiastic, but she did. She knew Faith had the ability to make even the most exciting fiesta sound like a parish council meeting.

She spent the rest of the afternoon, when she was supposed to be working, researching short trip travel opportunities to New York. Swallowing down the niggle of guilt she felt about not producing any copy, she consoled herself by booking a week's leave over Easter.

She expected Rufus to be late arriving home that evening, and started cooking dinner while mulling over her plans. She lit a perfumed candle, it made her feel that the apartment was somehow domesticated and homely with the light flickering. Then she switched her phone onto Spotify, pairing it with

Rufus's speaker. Humming along to her Dad's favourite, 'The Gambler' she was caught by the words 'know when to hold, know when to fold.' She stopped chopping onions and garlic and asked the kitchen at large, 'Should I hold or fold here? What did Granny ask me to do? I can fold now, say no more about it to anyone, but I'm sure there is a story to be told.'

Lizzie poured herself a small glass of red wine. Leaning back against the counter top she waved it ceremoniously, announcing, 'That woman didn't have my voice a century ago. She didn't have much of a voice at all, but I can do this for her. At least I can try. She must have been brave and frightened all at the same time. And she wasn't such a young girl either. Twenty-six I think, maybe she had a lover who wouldn't marry her? Well I know how that feels, don't I? Or maybe she was raped or coerced; being a servant, she would have been quite powerless if she'd been taken advantage of. Perhaps she was like the girl in the Skibbereen Eagle, totally her father's property. No "Me Too" movement in those days. Or maybe she just didn't know what she was doing?'

She took a swallow, draining the glass. She felt pleased and encouraged to have analysed her feelings and landed on the side of Ellen. Music and the slight sizzle of the perfumed candle made her happy and she made small two-step dance movements around the room.

The rattle of Rufus's key in the door brought her attention back to the onions. She quickly slung them into the cold frying pan and turned the heat up full.

'Hey Lizzie. How's it goin'? You cookin' tonight?'

'Observant of you, pal,' Lizzie responded, leaving the onions which were barely warm and turning her face towards Rufus, puckering her lips in a comic imitation of a kiss.

'Hmm. What are we having then, along with onions?'

'Oh, hadn't really decided Rufie. Maybe just it's a surprise.'

Rufus sighed and turned off the gas as the onions began to brown at the edges.

'Let's just go out, I fancy a pizza. An' you've a whiff of wine on your breath so I reckon it's not a school night.'

Her face broke into a smile, and she gave a small uplift to her shoulders as a response.

'You really don't enjoy cooking, do you kid? And I reckon you've had a bit of a lonely day.'

Lizzie's working from home days usually left her with cabin fever, and she generally went to the stables after work on those days. Rufus was surprised to see her at home until he noticed a printout of hotels in New York, which Lizzie had left on the table.

'What's all this, Liz? Thinking of going to New York?'

She felt unsure how to respond, caught out, unprepared.

'Faith thought it might be an idea for her and I to go to Ellis Island and see whether we could find out a bit more about Ellen. Did she go there or not? And if she did there will be loads of information…' her voice trailed away.

Rufus was looking at her, his face creased with amusement. He tried to hide it but his eyes always showed how he felt. That was one of the things she loved most about him. He really was completely transparent; she could read him like a very enjoyable book.

'What?'

'Faith thought, did she? Sounds like something we used to say at school: "a big boy told me to." Faith hasn't shown much interest in this great-grandmother bear hunt thing so far. Go on, tell your 'andsome.'

''Andsome indeed! Don't come all Cornish on me now. So, it's like this. I need to find out what happened to Ellen. No one else seems to have much of an idea and I just think she would have wanted me to tell her story.'

'Oh now Liz, come on. "She would have wanted." You have no idea what she would have wanted. You don't even know whether she wanted the child or not. Just imagine though, if she hadn't had the kid you wouldn't be here. That's a thought alright, isn't it?'

'Pizza, Rufus? And a bottle of red? My treat. I just want to talk it over with you, kind of explain how I'm feeling and the whole thing about the difference between then and now and I really want to get it straight in my head.'

Half an hour later, Lizzie and Rufus were settled in an Italian restaurant in Bedminster, the trendy cafe society area just around the corner.

Rufus was silent, scrutinising the menu. He kept his head bent when the waitress arrived to take their order.

'Can we just have a few minutes please, and a bottle of house red while we are making up our minds?'

'Sure. No problem. Get that for you now.'

'Don't please, Rufus. I'm tired hearing it.'

'Don't what, Liz? I'm just makin' up my mind here.'

'No, you're not. You're getting ready to be grumpy. First thing you'll say now is "No problem? Why should it be a problem?" then you'll say "Really a pizza is just a cheese sandwich isn't it?" What's up?'

'I feel left out, and that isn't like me at all. Why are you thinking of going to New York with your sister? Why aren't I going too?'

'It's a strange thing, Rufus. I feel as though this woman, Ellen..'

'She is Faith's great-great-grandmother, too.'

'Yeah. Well that's a bit the point. It feels like two women, her descendants, would understand her better even though it's a hundred and twenty years or so. And I think it will be a kind of bonding thing, for Faith and me. And I want to sink myself into her psyche if I can. If I can't then I want to know what it would have been like for her. I want to compare that to the lives Faith and I have here today. Do you get it?'

'Just New York, just for a few days. Reconnaissance?'

'Yup. Then I'll be home before you know it.'

'Actually, how about extending your trip, go on to New Orleans, I'll meet you there and we can have a few days of music and fun. You've always wanted to see New Orleans, now would be a good chance. Faith could fly back to Belfast on her own couldn't she?'

Lizzie leaned back as the wine arrived, grinning up at him "Andsome!'

'Oh, and a seafood pizza and side salad then please. With potato wedges.'

Returning home, Rufus threw his coat onto the sofa, causing Lizzie to wince; it was new, designer and cream. He strode across the compact room and perched his tall frame awkwardly onto her small swivel chair. The computer hadn't been closed down and he clicked onto the website she'd left open.

'Lucky I wasn't on a porn site, Rufie. No girl on girl action in sight. Disappointed?'

Rufus responded by waving his hand in the air, muttering, 'Coffee?'

Lizzie spooned coffee into the percolator and leaned against the kitchen counter waiting for the chocolate-nutty smell of coffee to fill the room.

Returning a few minutes later with two small glass cups she found him leaning back, arms clasped behind his head and a triumphant grin on his face.

'What?'

'Passenger lists. Look. Ship manifests. Not rocket science. You've paid the website, let them do the work.'

Leaving the coffee on the table, Lizzie bent over his chair. She inhaled the dusty smell of a man who'd spent his day calculating measurements on a draft board.

'What've you found, Rufie? Let me see.'

'A Cunard line ship, called *Caronia*, which sailed from

96

Queenstown in 1906, on 18 November, arriving seven days later at Ellis Island.'

'Let me get my magnifying glass. Oh look, here she is. She is here. Ellen Clancey. You are so clever!'

Rufus unwound from the legs up, leaving Lizzie to take his place on the chair.

'Yup I sure am. Took me the time it took you to make coffee. Ha. Should have been a detective, not an architect.'

'Love you, Rufie. Really do.'

'I'll get a chocolate with my coffee then, shall I? Genius that I am. Have to 'fess up kiddo. I'd been looking for this for a while, thought I'd found her earlier but didn't want to raise your hopes. Tonight seemed to be as good a night as any to surprise you!'

Lizzie was screwing her eyes at the screen, peering through the heavy lens of the magnifying glass No longer listening, she curtained the lens with her thick glossy brown hair. Rufus stroked her head, bending to give the back of her neck a kiss.

'She was going to stay with someone called Corrie Clancey and there's an address here and everything. I love her already, she's claiming to be twenty-nine, when I know for fact…'

'Fact?'

'Yes fact Rufus, I've seen her baptism registered in the church records. She's thirty-two if she's a day. Good woman!'

'Why would she lie, Liz?'

'I often lie about my age, and I certainly would if I was emigrating, leaving my past and family behind, and hoping to start a new life. Possibly a husband. And women always think men like them the younger the better.'

'That so? I'd better get a younger model then, you're knocking on a bit aren't you? Aren't you coming up thirty-two yourself?'

Lizzie flicked two fingers up at Rufus. They both laughed as she switched the computer onto sleep mode and followed him as he carried their coffee into the bedroom.

Chapter 12

Ellen. West Cork: October 1906.

'I must go now, Mam. I daren't stay any longer. An' I'm takin' Cathy with me.'

'You're mad, what's wrong with you, girl? I know you and Patrick were never a family, it was just the look of the thing, and well, so he's gone back to Cork. I'm sure maybe you are lonely sometimes. But we are all here, a family for ye. An' little Cathy, she's known nothing else, has she? Not really.'

'No, Ma. I know, but if I stay, I'm putting us all at risk. I've no choice, I have to go to America. An' I don't want too much said about it. In particular, I don't want you tellin' Hannah Daley.'

'What, that sneaky-eyed woman who used to be parlourmaid at Lahana House? What's it got to do with her, anyway?'

'Ma I'm tellin' ye. She's out to get me, so she is. An' if she does, it'll ruin us all.'

'She'll not ruin us, girl. She comes from a terrible family herself, an' no one with any sense would listen to her.'

'Well, I'm away out now Ma, Michael's taking me into Skibbereen town to see the agent. He's at Hosford's Store all day today but he won't be back again for another month and that might be too late.'

Ellen's heart was hammering so loudly she expected her mother to ask what the noise was. For five years she had hoped the deal between herself and Lady Berish was safe. Yesterday, Hannah Daley, the parlourmaid from her past, had reappeared.

Michael had written to her in Cork to say they had fired Hannah from the big house, she'd disappeared, left the area. Hadn't been heard of until suddenly, she came back.

She couldn't believe how suddenly her life had had to change again, but it felt just like the last time. She'd planned her escape then, knowing she had to be bold and quick. And she decided she'd do the same now.

Yesterday she'd been working in the potato field, helping Dada, picking after he turned the crop over. Back-aching, muddy work. Little Cathy, nearly five years old, had been playing with the sacks, stepping into them and hiding, keeping her eyes closed, thinking she couldn't be seen. Then Ellen had stood up to straighten her back, and heard a commotion on the far side of the lane. Hannah, hands on hip, was arguing with Michael.

Noticing her looking across, Michael had called out. 'Hey, Sissie. Can you get over here a minute. This one's causing trouble an' bad mouthin' ye.'

Ellen had worried about this for years. She knew Hannah's presence would be bad news. She'd been caught with Tom at Lahana just weeks before he was to marry Matilda Linehan. There had been a bit of a scandal, but one which was suppressed by Hannah's absence. The Berishes couldn't afford any whisper of indiscretion, not before their son was safely married to the heiress of Covamore House. She'd never been sure how much Hannah had known about her own arrangement with Tom's mother, but her habit of eavesdropping made it a risk.

Scooping Cathy up, she'd stepped carefully over the muddy, churned up field to the hedge which bounded the lane.

'Hush, me darling, I'll let you down in a minute, you're such a wriggler so ye are. Just like our Jimmy was at your age.'

Setting the child at her feet, brushing off some excess mud, she leaned into the hawthorn which covered the ledge of the drystone wall. She knew that boundary well and chose a patch of stone where the hedge was scant. A thick hessian sack, uniform amongst potato pickers, was pinned around her waist. It protected her from the jagged thorns, while her nervous fingers worried at the bright yellow pea-like hedge blossom. She tried to keep her face blank, hoping to cover the anxiety rippling just beneath her skin.

'What ails ye, Hannah? Have ye no work to do? Ye can come an' help us here if ye have a mind, can't she Michael?'

Michael had looked uncomfortable. He hadn't expected Sissie to offer Hannah a job. He'd hoped it was some girl thing and that he'd be free to get himself out of the way as soon as possible.

'I think Ellen knows well why I'm here, Michael. Shall I tell him, or will you do it yourself, "Sissie"?'

'Michael, can you take Cathy for a bit? Hannah and I have some women business to discuss, personal like, an' she's too young to hear it. Take her down to James, he's at the house and he loves to see her, and she him, don't ye darlin? Go an' see Uncle Jimmy, he's only here for the day, going back tomorrow.'

Michael's face flushed. No man wanted to be anywhere near the sort of talk that could be called women's business. Ellen had lifted her daughter over the hedge to Michael and watched as he hoisted her up onto his shoulders braying like a donkey, trotting them both down the lane to the farmhouse.

'Now what exactly can I do for ye, Hannah?'

'I'll come straight to the point, Ellen. I need money. An' I know you have plenty.'

'An' I'll come straight to the point too, Hannah, I owe you nothing. Whether I have money or no is not your concern, but I can assure you, you won't be seeing any from me.'

'Lady Berish came straight to the point five years ago, didn't she Ellen? Or Helen as she called you. Quite to the point. I heard it all. So if anyone finds out about your Cathy being Tom's little bastard...'

'Please don't use that word, Hannah.'

'If they do, then your lease on the farm will not be renewed and you'll pay her the money back or your family will carry the debt.'

Ellen's face had paled. This was her worst nightmare. If it had been anyone but Hannah she might have brushed the threat away. It was a long time ago, Tom was now married. He had two children with his wife, and whatever he got up to around the country nowadays was no longer news. She'd never been particularly fond of him. Flattered, she reckoned, just been a bit of fun, between the two of them. A brief few hours together, unexpected and unplanned. Unplanned by herself anyway."And all in all," she thought, "it was a good thing. I have Cathy. I love her beyond anything I could have ever imagined. Even more than I had loved Jimmy, still do love Jimmy, but not as fiercely as this."

'I can't give ye money, Hannah, I don't have any spare.'

'Liar. I know it. I've been living up in Cork and happened to meet Patrick Riley last week. He's after tellin' me ye kept him short when ye were in the city. Every penny had to be counted for. Never spent more than twelve pounds before ye came scurryin' back here to yer family, lettin' him sort himself out in the big city. Sure he's not got a penny to his name now.'

Hannah shook her head, implying a sadness for Patrick Riley that would have surprised him. He hardly knew her and she'd never shown him any interest before the chance encounter in Cork. Ellen felt her pulse quicken and her mouth dry as she listened, plucking feverishly at the yellow gorse blossoms.

'I know all about it, so I do,' Hannah continued, leaning in towards Ellen, too closely for her liking, recoiling as she caught a draft of sour breath.

'I was Tom's favourite for months on end, right up until he got sent away. An' now he's married to that English woman from Covamore, the great Linehan's daughter. Sure Tom's no good to me, hasn't been for years. He gave me some money, told me to go away, and it tided me over but now it's gone so I'm comin' to ye. Everyone has to look out for themselves, sure you know that Missus Ellen Clancey or Riley.'

'What is it you want from me, Hannah? I've very little to give but I could try an' get you a position somewhere. I'm sure Patrick would help, maybe Jimmy too. He's working in Dunmanway now, since he finished his schooling.' Hannah tilted her head like a bird checking for insects, but hoping for something more.

'He became a real scholar, y'know. His handwriting is just gorgeous and he can read right quickly. Cathy loves to hear him when he comes over home. They get on so well together, like brother and sister really.'

Hannah jerked her head up and looked Ellen in the face. 'Ha! Indeed. Well, they're not are they? Everyone knows that, even though your family has taken her in. Or are they "Sissie"? Can I call you that? I'd never thought on it before but maybe they are. You could be mother to them both. Ye were always that attached to him an' we heard about how you found money to let him stay on at school. Where'd that come from, eh?'

'Get out of my sight, Hannah, you really are too bold altogether.' Tears pricked Ellen's eyes, stung by the insult and the implied shame. 'Your stupid ideas, always trying to put the dirty mouth on everything. I'm going back to my work now. Shall I send my father after ye?'

'You've not heard the last of this, Ellen, Ellie, Helen, Sissie, whatever. I'll be back. It'll only take for me to drop a word into Lady Berish's ear an' you're done for.'

That had been nearly a month ago and now Ellen slumped against the hard upright wall of the overcrowded train carriage. The past weeks had been filled with arguments. Yelling, then hot tears which tore at her chest late into the night. How she hated conflict, she always considered she would know what was best for Cathy. But her mother had been unwavering.

'No, no, no.' She'd insisted. 'You do not take that child to Amerikay. You've nowhere to live, no idea about your future. Anyway, you won't be able to get work with a child around your ankles all day.'

'Then I won't go Ma, but I'm tellin' ye, there's risks involved in my stayin' an' if ye lose the farm, what then?'

Michael had been standing by the door, listening. He interrupted, holding his hand out palm forward to stop his mother from speaking. 'That Hannah girl has ye terrified Sissie, she won't say anything, you've given her a pound note, that's a month wages. Sure I saw ye meself. It was no "women's thing," secret.'

'She knows about the affidavit, Michael. An' if I go, she's no way to get any money, she knows it's me has it not the family. There'd be nothing more for her to squeeze once I'm away.'

'Well we need to make sure that if she does go Ma, Hannah'll not even know it 'til too late. We tell no one you'll be leavin', not even old Father Tomelty.'

'But Michael, I never expected it to come to this. All my plans for the future, Cathy and me. I thought maybe we'd just live here with ye all, or maybe get ourselves a place, maybe I'd marry…'

'Sure Sissie, no one will marry ye here, what're ye talkin' about?'

'Then could I not get a place of my own in Amerikay? I would pay rent, for a while at least.'

'Listen, Ellie, you're not thinking straight.' Her mother, having filled a teapot from the range kettle, reached for cups and set them on the kitchen table.

'No woman can set up on her own, and certainly not one without husband and a small child. Ye'd not just be an idle, with no future, no land, nothin'. Ye'd be taken for a fallen woman, so ye would.'

'Oh Mam, it's so hard, too hard. I don't think I can do right by you all. Look, please, I know I have to go, but if I do, will you make sure Cathy doesn't forget me. You will won't you, Ma? An' I'll be back for her soon as I can.'

The platform at Derryleague station had been crowded, heavy with emotion. Most people were leaving for a sailing to New York and would never return. She'd grown up knowing that to be a fact, everyone accepted it. But Ellen told herself she'd be back, just as soon as she got settled.

Now she watched the other emigrees, boarding late, not seeming eager to secure a space in the crowded carriage. The noise on the platform was riotous. There were women crying and making heartbreaking declarations of love, overlooked children protesting in degrees ranging from cranky complaints to ear-splitting wailing and everyone competing for attention.

Most passengers were surrounded by wide circles of well wishers, starting their farewells at the outer edge, making wild, unlikely promises. 'Sure I'll be back in no time at all, and the drinks are on me lads.' She knew the pattern, had seen it before, when neighbours had left. The fun and farewells of the American Wake soon forgotten in the cold reality of the morning departure. The traveller always moving towards the centre, where their closest kin, often the mother and father, stood caretaking their bundles of luggage. And she'd had no one to see her off. At least, not see her off with this level of desperation.

Her father and Michael had tacked up at first light and driven her to the station in the horse car. She'd left Cathy sleeping in the bed she shared with Mary Anne and Nora. The men had seen her into the carriage alright, but then she said they had to go.

Watching the outpourings, hugs and tears, followed by a reluctant tearing apart from loved ones, she wondered about the different reasons for their leaving.

The train had been impatiently puffing steam. Then it emitted a high-pitched screech, giving a final moment's notice of departure. As it pulled out of the station there were people running alongside the carriage, regardless of the speed or the steam catching their throats. She assumed they needed to be in sight of their departing ones until the last possible second.

She was alone and her heart felt ripped open. She remembered how her throat had lumped and her breath had been reluctant and slow as she'd signed the ship's ticket at Hosford's store. He was the main emigration agent in Skibbereen for the White Star line. The private back room behind the main grocery store had seen hundreds, if not thousands, of emigrants over the years. Although she'd felt sorry for herself, she was aware of how much worse it had been for those who had gone before her.

At least she had some trust in her future. Her daughter wouldn't starve to death and she wasn't facing the prospect, like those earlier generations, of dying on board the ship. Fifty years earlier and she might have been fleeing famine.

Archie O'Driscoll held the agency for the White Star Line, but she'd managed to buy a ticket for a Cunard sailing. His job was to handle the purchasing of tickets and the transport arrangements. He covered the whole area onto Queenstown Harbour and the sailings for New York. The Derryleague Post Office did have an agent, a man called Berish, but the name had put her off. Anyway, it was too close to home, she wanted to leave quietly.

One adult, steerage class SS *Coronia* to New York was what she had asked for. Agent O'Driscoll sold her a second class ticket – 'second cabin' he called it, an extra three pound up on steerage class. He'd said as she was a single woman she would be safer in second. And it would give her better food, a private bunk area and slightly more space. She'd also been told, but not promised, that on arrival, Ellis Island gave some preferential treatment to second class over steerage passengers.

She hadn't wanted to pay for second class and resented the additional cost. Agent O'Driscoll told her there was a waiting list for steerage, or she could go standby. He also offered her the option of going to Berish in Derryleague but he didn't think there would be any spare tickets for a couple of months. There hadn't been much choice.

She'd found it difficult to sign the document confirming payment through blurred eyes brimming with tears. It wasn't the going to America that bothered her, it was the "one adult".

'How much for a child?' she'd asked.

'Three pound for second cabin. Do ye have a child, missus?'

'I do. But my father has refused to let me take her with me.'

'And your husband, the child's father? Is he dead?'

'Yes.' Looking up, Ellen caught the glimpse of disbelief hovering around the man's eyebrows. 'Very dead.' She dared him to smirk. He didn't.

'Then I'm afraid it's down to your father to say whether you can take the child out of the country or not. He is the head of your household and the minor is in his charge. You don't need his permission to travel yourself, of course, the age you are. You'll soon get employment and you will remember to send the postal orders back now, won't you?'

His patronising tone stung her pride, but she couldn't resist asking, 'D'ye know much about it, Amerikay? We hear plenty from neighbours about how they want women as servants in New York and pay good money. I'll need to get set up as soon as I can. Then see if Dada will change his mind about letting the child come over.'

'Well, I hear no more than you do, missus. You can read and write, so yes, you should do very well. Speaking English too, not like some people they have going over these days. Italians, Jews, whatnots. They like servants who can manage the grocery lists and not be cheated out of their money by the shopkeepers.

That's the credit of the National School for us now. And for sure, we've not much need for servants around here ourselves, now have we?'

While he was shuffling through the papers, preparing her tickets and acting as officiously as a bishop, Ellen had let her mind wander away from Skibbereen, away from worrying about whether the neighbours might see her, away from Hannah Daley. By horse car, rail, boat, and then where? She didn't know. But America seemed the safest place to head for.

Her uncle Corrie was in New York. She'd write to him, once the ticket was in her hand, asking him to take her in until she could get herself settled. There had been no time to lose. She just didn't dare wait the weeks it would take until she'd get a reply. She was going under an assumption that it would simply have to work out.

'Will you sign this now, please?' It wasn't really a question, she'd already signed one document, this was his copy.

'And now, have you the money for me? There'll be no refund if you fail to make the train or the sailing arrangements. Understood?'

'No doubt about it, sir.' She'd thought he'd like the title, suggesting deference, and the shadow of a smile flitting across his dry, bland face had confirmed it.

'I need the earliest sailing I can get,' she'd told him. 'There won't be an American Wake for me, it's not widely known that I am leaving. I'll take it that this conversation and my arrangements are confidential.'

Hosford's shop front, with it's clearly displayed White Star Agent board leaning against its front window, was right on Bridge Street. But it was also a general store. Ellen shrugged off the worry of being seen, deciding it more than likely she'd be taken for a groceries shopper.

Agent O'Driscoll didn't respond, or give any sign he had heard the question at all, and he'd continued giving instructions.

Ellen had thought his evasiveness matched his bishop-like looks.

She'd leaned forward and listened. Every muscle, back, shoulders, even her buttocks clenched, intent. She had to be on her guard, couldn't afford to get this wrong, but she seldom confused important details, although sometimes dates and numbers were difficult.

'SS *Caronia* sails on 18th November. Next week. Take the train from Derryleague, it leaves at seven in the morning, gets you into Cork at nine. Change in Cork for a train to Queenstown Harbour. Shouldn't take more than an hour and a half. But do allow yourself a bit of time, you don't want to be late and the place will be crowded. Be at the quay, Cunard is alongside the White Star, be ready for the tender. It leaves at two in the afternoon. You'll see grand signs up everywhere with the names of the different ships. You must look out for the name *Caronia*. She won't be the only ship leaving.'

Ellen nodded, sitting back in her chair and opening her handbag in anticipation of the next step.

'I have it all written down here now for ye. May I request payment now please missus?'

She handed over the eight pound notes, counting them as she laid them on the highly polished counter. It was nearly a servant's wage for a year and it hurt to have her carefully guarded pot diminished.

'Thank you, well explained. I will be really upset leaving them all and I've never been further than Cork,' she said, laying the notes down. 'I've a friend there.'

Ellen gasped as she said that. She hoped he hadn't heard. Patrick Riley, the one person who possibly could give her permission to take the child was still, as far as she knew, in Cork. She resisted the urge to say to Agent O'Driscoll, 'Of course, he could be very dead by now.'

She didn't reckon the man had a sense of humour, her

position was precarious and there was no need to raise any complication.

He'd told her to check the newspaper for confirmation that the ship had left Liverpool to cross the Irish sea to Queenstown. She had cycled into Derryleague every day to read the paper. When the sailing was recorded, she knew that her exile had begun.

Chapter 13

Ellen. Queenstown & SS Caronia: November 1906.

Ellen had no problem tolerating the crowded train. She knew it was another life changing event, but she was getting used to those. Settling into a no-going-back calm, she joined the struggling, bustling, near panicking mass of people changing at Cork onto the Queenstown train. Hunched in the corner of the overfilled carriage, suitcase at her feet, she intended to be apart, alone.

An air of sadness shrouded the streets of Queenstown. It reminded her of dolorous Good Fridays when people fasted and prayed all day. A thick cloak of sorrow, impossible to shake off, permeated every brick and tile, the buildings seemed to be holding the memory of those who had left.

The incomplete, not yet consecrated, cathedral of St Colman dominated the sloping hill above the town. Fifty years it had been in the building of this elaborate church. Ellen frowned, thinking about the effort and funds that had been spent on its construction. 'Would have been better used to reduce the misery and hunger which was all around in those years,' she muttered.

Walking towards the harbour she shivered, looking at the tall, narrow four-storey houses which clutched its three sides. She'd been told they were crammed tight with emigrants awaiting departure. There had been plenty of stories back in

Derryleague about the bleak cold rooms, and no one expected them to be clean.

Ellen had no desire to explore the sights of the town and waded, hauling her suitcase through the crowd, over to the quayside.

The Cunard Warf was easy to find, although less imposing than its neighbour the White Star. The gold bird-like insignia on the flag flapped like a trapped chicken on the flagpole above the crowd. A white-columned customs house, its tall masts decked out in multicoloured bunting, surrounded the harbour entrance. As Ellen walked towards a low red brick building with the words Cunard painted in six foot high lettering along the side, she saw the *Caronia* waiting. Twin funnels were steaming. There was a mighty tension coming from within the body of the ship and *Caronia* was impatient to be released.

An Irish November day is always cool, although there was a shimmer of sunshine struggling though heavy grey clouds. The wind coming off the sea, causing the waves to chop, had lowered the temperature. Ellen shivered. She'd dressed in all her winter clothes, leaving suitcase space for her belongings. She mentally checked the contents while she leaned against the red brick wall. A washbag and towel, a spare pair of shoes, two summer dresses, some underwear. That was all she owned. Mam had given her a small package of Clonakilty black pudding for Uncle Corrie. It lay at the bottom of her case, wrapped in waxed paper, securely tied with string. She'd also taken a small cardboard box containing Cathy mementos – her baby gown and recently outgrown boots.

A sling, made of an old pair of outworn breeches of her fathers, lay across her chest, under her coat. Her handbag, money and ship's tickets kept safe. She'd also brought the affidavit from Lady Berish, and Cathy's birth certificate. She'd taken those in case she ever needed to prove where her funds or her child had come from. The reassuring weight comforted her, safe from any pickpocket or accidental loss.

Her stomach growled and she unwrapped the bread and cheese brought from home. The harbour wall gave her shelter from the wind and she munched on the dry food until hearing the announcement to board the tender.

Once on the ship she soon found her sleeping quarter, following the number registered on her ticket. Her tight boots were calling for attention and, sighing with relief, she eased her feet out. Massaging them through her thick woollen stockings as she sat on the narrow bed, she fought against the urge to lie down. She didn't plan to miss the first meal in the dining hall.

Checking the lock on her door, she stowed the suitcase under her bed, reluctantly pulling boots on over her sweating feet. Unsure of how to approach the dining hall, she counted the steps up the steep iron staircase, following the smell of food.

Never having eaten a meal with strangers, she hoped she'd find out how to behave by watching. Her family, and the servants in the Lahana House kitchen, were the only people with whom she'd ever shared food. Michael had told her of the habits at the serving tables with the Berish family, but she'd never been around when they were eating.

Her eyes widened. A line of passengers had formed along one side of an enormous dining hall, carrying their trays, facing a counter of steaming food more plentiful than she'd expected. There had been no instructions, but she had brought her ticket and noticed that they were being checked.

The queue snaked three sides of the room and she hoped there would be enough to go round. Not having enough to go round had often happened at Lahana, the result of arriving late. She worried that not having a timepiece might be awkward. She could tell the time, learned from reading her father's fob watch but other timings went by indications from weather, body signals or observing others. She had always relied on having help with timings, and knew she would miss not having anyone around to set her right.

Moving into the line, she noticed a couple of passengers squeeze in behind her. A pale clean shaven man, looking younger than herself, dressed in a quality woollen suit and a linen shirt with a stiff collar. She reckoned he'd probably put the outfit on for the journey. The woman at his side was wearing a headscarf and hugged a woollen shawl across her narrow chest. The lower half of her body was concealed, tucked inside a wide thick skirt, topped off by a linen apron. Ellen suspected that the skirt covered at least one petticoat. She expected that the woman was storing their valuables under her apron.

'D'ye mind me askin', but is this where we eat our food every day and is it about this time?' Ellen asked.

'Good evening, missus,' the unfamiliar accent was a surprise. He made a short stiff bow from the waist as he spoke, without removing his trilby. The woman looked nervous. She didn't offer a response, but gave Ellen a hesitant smile, looking to her husband for approval.

'We ate here four times in the day, surprisin' though it may seem. I've never ate more than twice in a day before so it's somethin' of a shock to yer system I can tell ye. We're from Belfast oursel's, so we are. But we boarded at Liverpool, an' we're well used to the routine. We can offer ye some advice, if ye want it that is.'

'Sure that would be lovely, sir. My name's Ellen Clancey, and I just boarded there at Queenstown.'

'Well, the ship's bell will ring four times and if ye be after hearin' it, come straight to this wee place and get yersel' into the queue. Always bring yer ticket with ye mind, and make sure ye lock yer cabin door before ye come up. That's about it, so it is.'

'An' my name's Bessie,' the wife said. Her small voice fitted her demeanour. 'An' my husband here, Gerald, Mr. Gerald Cummings, well we've been tryin' our luck in Liverpool, but the work's scarce there, hardly better than at home, so we've took our chance at Amerikay.'

Ellen smiled, pleased that here was an introduction. She felt less alone as she edged her way forward along the creeping line. They carried their trays onto one of the long bench seats which bordered refectory-style tables. Their company, although quiet and reserved, was a relief to Ellen. In the days before she left she'd been wary of any probing, however incidental. She had spent so much time thinking about how she might avoid awkward questions that eating her meal and not needing to be thinking about too much conversation suited her.

She looked up when she heard Gerald say, 'We'll see ye in the morning, so we will. Listen for thon wee bell now and I hope yer sleep doesn't be too disturbed by this rough sea.'

He pushed back his chair, having finished his meal, ignoring Bessie, who was still eating. Ellen dropped her gaze, careful to avoid eye contact. She noticed Bessie folding her bread around a sausage. She placed it into the pocket of her apron before rising to join her husband.

Over the next few days Bessie, Gerald and herself looked out for each other in the food queue, selecting a table that would have space for all three. Her mood lifted, she no longer felt alone. Even her self-doubt began to fizzle away.

'Well, I managed fine in Cork,' she reminded herself. She'd made all the arrangements for herself and Patrick. From buying the second hand wedding ring to convincing the landlady they were Mr and Mrs Riley. 'I can't see as Bessie would do that.' She'd had to make a decision about Cathy's name too. They had registered her as Catherine Riley, Patrick had kept his word.

'I can do it, ye know.' She announced to Bessie and Gerald halfway through their dinner on the second day, 'I can manage in Amerikay. It won't be so very different from Cork after all.'

They looked up at her, Gerald chewing thoughtfully on the fattened end of belly pork, unable to speak, while Bessie, although her mouth was free, remained silent. Ellen noticed that Bessie rarely spoke before her husband.

'I've an uncle meeting me in New York, at least if he don't meet me I have his address. An' I can read and write, Irish and English, so I can. I'm expectin' to get work as a servant in a fine New York house, make my money, then come back for my child.' Gerald spluttered, half choking on his belly pork. He took a swig of water before responding, his eyes watering and his lips smeared with grease.

'New York, I can tell ye, is not one bit like Cork. Have ye no heared tell o' the tall buildings would crack yer neck ter look at them. An' there's all sorts there, not just Irish into the United States, but Italians, Jews, Hungarians, Germans. Did ye not know that, missus?'

Ellen nodded as though accepting what Gerald said, but giving it little weight, knowing he'd never been to America.

'Well, sure, I'll take my chance with them, so. An' are they good with children is what I want to know. I'm bringing my daughter over next year, or maybe it will be the year after, depends how the money goes, really.'

'Aye, they might be good with weans alright, but they won't want yours. With or without a Da.' He looked at her through narrowed eyes. It was the first time she had mentioned Cathy, and she wasn't sure whether she should have pretended to be a widow.

'They want workers, labourers men and servants women. That's what we'll all be registered as, whatever our skills or learnin' is. An' I'll tell you somethin' else fer nothin'. They'll not be payin' enough ter travel back to the old country within the next five or ten years, that's for sure.'

Ellen bit her lip, hard, to prevent herself responding. She wasn't going to let him know she had money, and she'd prove him wrong. But this wasn't good news. She reckoned Gerald had had a tough time in Liverpool and was portraying a future grimmer than it needed to be. Perhaps, she thought, he wanted his wife to appreciate the difficulties ahead.

She hadn't known what to expect on board, but she soon got used to the constant rolling motion. 'It's the reciprocating engines', Gerald had informed her when she'd asked about the throbbing noise which became more noticeable towards the aft of the ship.

'No idea what they are Gerald, but anyways, long as it's normal, I won't worry. Wakes me up in the night though.'

He'd puffed up a bit when she said that, straining the buttons on the worn linen shirt which had long since replaced the suit, explaining facts in a slow and careful voice. Ellen wondered did he think she was a simpleton. Of course she knew that a ship moved with the waves, up and down. It was only to be expected. 'An' it might get a whole lot worse before it gets better,' he warned.

Her only symptom had been a slight queasiness caused by the smell of cooking wafting into her cabin, which was downwind of the galley.

Most afternoons she lay stretched out on the bed in her 'second cabin'. The room was the same size as the one she'd shared with her sisters and Cathy at home. The women's washing facilities down the corridor were clean. All round it was more sophisticated than she had expected.

On the first morning at sea she'd found the bath-steward and arranged a bath time for later that day.

'A full bath to myself and no one waitin' to use the water,' she'd marvelled, pouring a jugful of hot water over her head. 'This electricity is powerful good altogether. I'm sure I'll have a come down when I get settled, it won't be like this everywhere. But anyway, that's a worry for another day.'

Agent O'Driscoll had painted an exaggeratedly grim picture of the steerage class facilities. 'In steerage the toilet facilities are not segregated at all and once the washing vessels run out the floors will be clotted with vomit.' His tone had been grim, almost funereal, as he concluded 'in between sanding down, of course.'

A sorrowful smile had crossed his bishop-like face before he offered his final sliver of foreboding. 'You'd expect sickness in the middle of the ocean, in November. It'll be rough, missus.'

It had made the option of the second cabin ticket more attractive and now she felt the benefit. Six days on board were spent exploring the three year old ship, which was finished more elegantly than anything Ellen had seen in Lahana House. She wandered through rooms edged by gleaming mahogany wood panelling, thinking, "I wonder who has to do the polishin' and dustin' in here? Sure it's grand altogether, being on the other side of all that housekeepin'."

Settling herself, most evenings, into one of the deep leather armchairs of the Ladies Reading Room, she'd pick up and then put down without reading, the Liverpool Daily Post or the Sunday Independent, from Cork. Both papers were out of date and her gaze travelled over the other women passengers. They seemed exotic, more colourful and varied than the company she had been used to.

One evening she sat with Bessie and between them they tried to follow snatches of conversation. 'Bessie,' she leaned across and whispered in reading-room hush, 'some of these accents are difficult to follow. They are sharper and faster than the Cork voices.'

'Well Ellie, being as this sailing began in Liverpool and Queenstown was the only other stop before New York, they has to be English.'

'Tis my second language, so. I'm finding the Irish north and Scotland really hard to follow too.' Grinning, she put her arm around Bessie. 'Luckily enough, I've been broken in like one of Dada's donkeys by talking with your good self and Gerald.'

She could pick out sentences of hardship: 'when we lost her and the baby', 'died for want of a roof over their heads'. Then there were beliefs in a better future, these were frequent.

Mostly she heard 'there is a good life waiting for us once we're landed' and 'know this will be a grand future too'.

But mostly, Ellen, the farm girl, wanted to gulp the open air: wild and salty, rough and grey. She needed the outdoors. Making her way up to the second cabin deck every morning she found enough space to choose a sheltered hideaway near the stern. She liked to stand alone on deck, watching the couples and family groups clustering together or walking around the ship. Everyone scanning the horizon.

She'd picked out the spot on the second morning at sea. They'd just passed Ireland's Teardrop, Fastnet Rock. The new lighthouse an upright pillar, puncturing the horizon. It warned of danger to shipping, she'd read about it on the ship's daily bulletin board. The island was seven miles out from Cape Clear, not too distant from the village of Baltimore, which in turn was close to Skibbereen. She'd stayed once, visiting an aunt who lived there, it was well known for fishing and a good harbour for imports. 'I'll pass you again soon enough, Teardrop,' she'd promised herself. 'I'll pass you on my way back and in a happier time.'

No one was within earshot, so she'd chanted under her breath, half a song, half a prayer, 'Oh for sure, I'll be back. Oh for sure, I'll be back. I'll be back for you my little one and I'll be back.' Her urge to celebrate was strong, and she gave small jigging steps in time to the words. Then she took a deep breath of sea air looking behind as though the last glimpse of county Cork would hear her and the message be received. 'Do yer best, Hannah. Ye' can't get to me now.'

Six days later the ship arrived into the harbour in New York. Ellen stood amongst the crowd of first and second-class passengers who had packed the deck since daybreak. Their eyes strained as the outlines of the New York buildings, irregular and tall, grew close, causing a ripple of exclaiming to run through the passengers.

'I'm sure you'll be lookin' out fer the Statue of Liberty.' She recognised Gerald's voice but didn't turn her head. 'It's the most famous landmark, so it is. Our fortunes are just waitin' for us!'

'Yes, Gerald. I've heard tell of it. 'Tis said to offer liberty and comfort to all who sail to the new world.'

Gerald's remarks brought to mind her father telling of his brother Corrie, the uncle she hoped to meet, proudly showing his ticket around before he left. 'My father told me of tickets printed with the promise "I'll be digging for gold!"'

'And you are too, wee woman, you are too.'

'Well, I know gold was what they came for forty years ago Gerald, but I've no expectation myself. Safety for sure and somewhere I could make a home, a family even.'

Gerald put his hand on her shoulder before turning down the staircase, muttering something about seeing how Bessie was feeling.

Looking around she saw people tightening their postures, standing more upright as they leaned against the railings, anxious to see their destination.

She'd rarely spoken to them, but their faces had become familiar during the past week, and, whether crew or passenger, they were her community at sea. She felt sad at the thought of losing contact and starting again. Looking around she noticed that people were leaving the deck, before returning back up the stairway in fresh clothes. She could see how best outfits were being worn for arrival. Clean long skirts, neat overjackets or shawls, hair fashioned into elaborate buns, hats pinned on or clutched in hand, they all seemed to be ready to disembark in style.

She made her way down to her cabin, scolding herself, 'I've nothing to put on. I have what I'm wearing and I've been wearing it for a week. Lucky I had the two hot baths but I reckon the dress, it'll smell desperate.' The scolding didn't last, she soon had a plan. 'The hair now, I can do something here.' Her dark curls had been a nuisance during the voyage. Never tame, they had reacted to the ocean air like drying seaweed and haloed her round dimpled face in a dark frothy mass.

Amongst her washing paraphernalia, she found half a dozen hair clips and a comb. Clutching these she strode down the corridor to the women's washroom. She knew she didn't have to book a bathroom just for the sink, and plunged her head under the tap.

She let out a small cry as the cold water ran over the back of her neck, drenching her thick curls. Tossing her head back she spent five minutes harshly combing. 'I daren't take longer, don't want to miss out on first sight of the statue. Indeed, an' I don't want to miss the instructions of what to do when we get there so I don't.' Her reflection in the pockmarked mirror above the basin looked less like a wild farm girl and more like the tame servant. 'I'm certainly planning on lookin' respectable,' she muttered, twisting and pinning her hair onto the top of her head in a knot.

Chapter 14

Lizzie and Faith. New York: April 2023.

Lizzie bought two black tee shirts with a silver motif of a Manhattan skyline and the words "New York" in glittery art deco style across the front.

Wearing hers, she handed a paper bag to Faith as soon as they met in Heathrow Airport's busy departure lounge.

'What's this, little sis? Is it your personal luggage label, in case you get lost or forget where we are going?'

'Come on, Faith, just a bit of fun. Put yours on too. Please, just for me!'

'I suppose you bought me an extra large and yourself a wee small one, did you?'

'Well, yes, actually. It's only cheap, from Peabodys, you don't need to wear it all the time.'

Faith's expression contorted into a comic frown and her lips puckered in an exaggerated pout. She slipped the tee shirt over her head, pulling her arms through the wide sleeves.

'Right, we're off to the bar Faith, I'm buying. We need Prosecco.'

Armed with two glasses of the trademark sparkling wine which, they reckoned, defined an event as celebratory, they settled in the corner of the airport bar.

'How's Mum?' Lizzie had been monitoring her internal emotional hourglass. Whilst she was rapidly filling up with feeling for Ellen, she wasn't growing any closer to her mother.

'Same as ever, really. Demanding. But since Gran died, she's been more sociable and has friends round a bit. She's taken up walking again and golf, so that takes the pressure off me.'

Lizzie took a sip and waited. She knew Faith's pauses often presaged the information she wanted to share. She swallowed a few more sips.

'Oh. And. I've met someone.'

'Faith, you dark horse. Tell me more.'

'Nothing more to say, really.'

'And?'

'Our headmaster, actually. Lost his wife to cancer a year ago and we've always had a good relationship.'

'Go on.'

'Not funny. You look at me like that, wide eyed and suspicious.'

'No. It's just you using that word. Relationship. Facebook status?'

'A good working relationship, I mean. I never knew his wife, never met them socially at all.'

'So? Don't tell me. You were on Tinder?'

'No Lizzie, just a fundraising walk for cancer.'

'Oh, just a fundraising walk for cancer and then you got off with him?'

'Don't be daft. We all went, the entire school. We had cars at either end of the trail. Then I ended up giving him a lift back in mine, and we just got on. Started with a few walks, not sure if they were dates, but anyway, there you are.'

'Name?' Lizzie leaned over the table, she wasn't going to let this go.

'Why?'

'Well he must have one, and I will meet him, won't I?'

Faith wriggled uncomfortably on her padded plastic seat, looking around as though hoping there might be an escape.

'Martin. Don't know, maybe.'

'Are you happy, Faith?'

'So, I'm wearing the silly tee shirt, I'm drinking Prosecco, I'm telling you about my private life. What do you think about that?'

'Love you, Faith. You deserve every bit.'

'And what about you, sister dear. How's your life?'

Lizzie leaned back, finishing her drink, and rolling the stem of her glass between her palms, taking her time to reply.

'Well, I'm wearing the tee shirt too. But I'm not sure where we are going, Rufus and me. He's fun and kind, and I think he loves me alright. But we do our own thing, you know. We never get further along.'

'And what do you actually want?'

'Well, actually, I enjoy being free and attached at the same time. I earn more than enough money to keep myself. I've loads of interests and friends which don't include him. I go to the stables, he doesn't like horses. He plays badminton, I hate sweaty sports. He clicks his camera, I'm happy to post and tweet. We have a good life together, so why not?'

'Cheers to both our lifestyles then, Liz. Shall I get us another?'

'Yes, definitely Faith, you are a changed woman alright!'

As Faith took away their empty glasses, Lizzie looked around the bar. Although she would describe it as American bar it was only slightly more atmospheric than the main concourse.

There was plenty of opportunity to people watch. She'd always enjoyed glimpsing into other lives, which she considered gave her an intuitive edge to her journalism.

The couple at a nearby table caught her attention. The man was slightly built, wearing an open-necked shirt revealing a clavicle-stopped tan. He was concentrating on his tablet, which rested in an Alexander Wang cover. She recognised the expensive trademark logo, and couldn't help feeling impressed. He lifted his head as each new customer entered the area. Sometimes the glance lingered, sometimes it did not. She sensed, by the irritated tapping of glossy red fingernails on the table top, that his companion knew what he was doing. She would know there was an attractive newcomer nearby without having to look.

'Two Proseccos, Lizzie. Here, can you take yours? Bar was busy.'

'Faith, see them over there. Loaded. He scores the women as they come in, a long linger or a short linger. I'm going to walk across the floor now, go to the loo maybe, see if I catch his eye. If I do Faith, will you count how long he looks at me? Go on, do. Just for a giggle.'

'Ok, I'll do it. Let's see you turn a head.'

Lizzie laughed gently, shaking her head, pouting and clinking her glass against her sister's.

'Nah. Only kiddin', Faith. I'm happy enough as I am. Cheers for the drink by the way.'

At the sound of their conversation, the man looked up, caught her eye and lingered for quite a few seconds. Maybe, she hoped, it was happiness rather than looks which attracted him. Suddenly shy, she looked away.

Faith, watching with an amused smile, muttered, 'You always get the attention. Don't you know that by now?' By way of response, Lizzie slid a dog-eared travel brochure, recommending the sights of New York, across the shiny surface of the bar table.

'Our two o'clock flight gets us in at four-ish Faith. The time lag works in our favour, so I've booked a table in a sports bar near our hotel for an early dine. We'll be shattered but the best way to cope with jet lag is just keep going. Hope you don't mind, it will be raucous.'

'I'll cope, sister. Looks like you've done a bit of homework here. What comes next then?'

'Ellis Island. Can't wait.'

'I can. Most people think the big thrill is the Statue of Liberty, but no such touristy glamour for us, eh?'

Lizzie gabbled, excitement bubbling through her sentences, facts tumbling out one over another.

'It's unbelievable really, Faith. That immigration depot was up and running between 1892 and 1954. They processed twelve million immigrants seeking a new life.'

Faith raised a quizzical eyebrow, seeming unimpressed.

'Processed? Like cheese? Really Liz, you have a way with words for a journalist. Please do me the courtesy of remembering I have a degree in history. I have heard about it. You'll be describing the Statue of Liberty to me next!'

'Well, anyway, I booked online. "To avoid the queues", they said. I plan for us to spend as long as possible on the island. We can retrace Ellen's footsteps and get an overall sense of the size of the programme.'

Faith nodded. By the time their flight had been called and they'd boarded, they were mellow and relaxed.

On landing, they managed the transition through the airport with little official interruption. Facemasks on and temperatures taken, but the taxi rank moved quickly and they were out in the city in a few minutes.

Sitting side by side at the back of a New York yellow cab, they were silent, until they sighted a famous landmark. 'Sure it's like an American movie, the way Brooklyn Bridge is lit up over there.'

'An' I'm loving the way the cab lights flash over rusting fire escapes. They look as though they've grown out of the walls of these brownstones.'

'Brownstones! Did you get than from watching *Friends*, Liz?'

'Glitzy lights of Fifth Avenue approaching. And I'm ignoring that last wee remark, Faith. I'll put it down to jet lag!'

Faith squeezed her arm and murmured, 'I can't believe that this six-hour journey would have taken Ellen six days. She'd have had very little chance of ever coming home. The poor critter.'

'I was just thinking how much it would have changed, Faith. One hundred and twenty years, it's a long time alright. And now we consider it as a mini break, can come again if we want to. It's amazing.'

'Actually, I think we should thank her. She's brought us here, and I'd never have come otherwise.'

Lizzie smiled, with a responding squeeze. 'It's not about New York; it's about family ties and who knows what we will find here?'

The next morning they took a cab to Battery Park. Lizzie insisted on the extravagance, pushing her card into the meter and shaking her head at Faith, who was tentatively holding out a ten-dollar bill.

Joining the straggling line of tourists hugging takeaway coffee cups, they wandered towards the terminal gate, where an imposing white tent bordered the waterside. Passing signs asking whether passengers were carrying dangerous weapons like knives or guns, and going through the metal detectors made a dent in their bubbly mood. They wordlessly handed over bags and coats to the uniformed staff at the security counter. Then, filled with anticipation, they boarded the ferry.

Ten minutes out onto the Hudson the engine slowed and they moved closer to the base of the Statue of Liberty, the first stop. Half of the passengers disembarked, the remainder came alive as if by some invisible signal. Most of the passengers were shrieking excitedly, clicking cameras and phones and holding up selfie sticks.

Neither of them had said anything about seeing the monument, but the change in atmosphere which overwhelmed the deck encouraged them to move forward. Leaning against the railings, they watched the ferry tourists move up the arrivals ramp before the rope drop allowed the contraflow to pile on board.

'Maybe everyone except us feels they don't get their money's worth unless they've bagged the shots, Lizzie.'

'I've stopped taking photos. Rufus always does it but maybe today…'

'Yes, maybe today we will.'

Lizzie chewed her bottom lip as they drew close to Ellis Island. The imposing red brick front of the main arrivals building, flanked by four turrets, dominated the quayside. It looked both menacing and reassuring.

'What do you think, Faith? Scary or safe?' Lizzie turned to her silent sister, who quickly brushed the back of her hand across her eye.

Lizzie put her arm around her. 'It's alright, Faith. It's fine to feel overwhelmed by all this. It was massive, what she did, and I'm not sure I could have coped.'

'Oh, you'd have coped, Liz. Some man would have taken you on and you'd have had a new life in no time at all. But I'm not sure about Ellen.'

'No, I'm not either, Faith. I've yet to see a photograph of her but she wouldn't have been a raving beauty or I think somewhere in the family memoirs that would have been mentioned. And she was a single woman with a child and not much money. We know she could read and write, in two languages, so she wasn't uneducated. But she must have been unworldly. She's in for a shock or two when she gets here, that's for sure.'

Faith's brow twitched irritably as she heard her sister using the present tense to refer to Ellen's arrival. 'I hate it when you make assumptions, Liz. I hate when you do that. Totally carried away.'

Queuing to get off the ferry onto the forecourt of the arrivals terminal, then up the wide stone steps, took a few minutes. Stepping into a vast atrium with imposing high ceilings and gleaming polished floors, Lizzie shivered. She turned to her sister. 'I can already sense the tension. It's as though these walls with their "hopes and tears" motto contain the anxieties of the thousands who've passed through.'

'Five hundred thousand a year, Liz.'

'I know Faith, it's amazing. I want to walk where they walked and feel what they felt, so I do.'

Lizzie raised her voice and threw both arms in the air. Her handbag slipped down to her shoulder, blocking the pathway of a small boy heading towards the souvenir shop. He stumbled and stopped, looking up at her. Backing away slowly, she felt a wash of guilt. Her Northern Ireland-British accent would have been strange to the child but more likely, she thought, the decisiveness of her announcement had taken him by surprise.

Faith snorted. 'Cool it wee woman. He's going to put his hands in the air any minute and you're going to find yourself in trouble. I wouldn't think they tolerate too much messing here.'

Lizzie sighed. 'I'm moved, that's all it is, Faith. I can feel the sense of desperation and hope and I want Ellen to be alright.'

'You know she was alright, Liz. She's on the ship's manifest. And you know she got in. Being a bit dramatic here, I think.'

Climbing the stairs from the arrivals to the baggage hall, they moved slowly. They read the huge white boards which hung on the walls. These represented the places where medical inspectors would have stood, marking the coats of immigrants with white chalk.

'Picking out those for medical examination, Liz. X for mental instability, L for lung problem, H for heart. I wonder did they also have a wee code of their own, GLW or FLK?'

'Oh, you are heartless Faith, Good Looking Woman or Funny Looking Kid? Maybe it is the gene pool they are interested in! Look what this says: Some immigrants realised what was happening and if marked took their coats off before entering the examinations hall. I'm sure Ellen would have done that.'

'Well yes, but she wasn't ill, was she? Or were you thinking GLW? Just please stop being so fanciful, Lizzie. It's all getting a bit much.'

Faith turned around to see her response, but her sister had already crossed the room. She was staring at an interactive screen with a push button test.

Sighing, she walked over to where Lizzie was doing small jumping movements in front of the machine. 'Are you going to be like this all day?' she asked. 'A scampering puppy newly released from quarantine.'

'Look at this, Faith; I can input her details and this will tell me whether she will be accepted or rejected. Single woman, check, No spouse, check, Male relative...'

'Go on Liz, put "yes".'

'Accepted.'

'Know what Liz, this woman is tough. She's travelling on her own and she's hoping a male relative is going to take her in. She's driven alright.'

'Don't know where she could have got that from Faith, do you?'

'Should have called you Ellen!'

'No, Faith, you're the sensible one, so more like you actually.'

Moving through to the exhibition room, they browsed the walls papered with black and white photographs. There were Poles, Jews, Czechs, Italians, all with frightened solemn faces. Towards the end of the last wall, Lizzie stopped and called out, not too loudly but with rising excitement making her voice squeak.

'That's her, Faith. That's definitely her.'

'For heaven's sake, Liz. It says "Irish Servant, 1906".'

'Yes, I know, and that was what she was. She looks about mid-twenties, doesn't she? Although we know she's really thirty-two. And all the family have that wonderful dark hair. And look at her, don't you feel you know her?'

'No, actually, I don't but if you do, well fine. She looks well dressed, strong and confident. Let's have her, shall we?'

Lizzie smiled when she heard Faith's response, a smile which deepened when she felt her arm being linked. They meandered through the remaining exhibits, on their way to the registry room, where the futures of immigrants were decided.

'D'you think all this is for real, Faith?' she asked, stopping in front of a poster advertising work, citing agents and their contact details. 'It's feeling too good to be true. Interpreters being lenient with translation, food, and medical care being provided for those whose processing has been delayed. Seems like they really valued them.'

'Yeah, but look here. They're letting their own countrymen in, sometimes even loaning them money. Now no-one is that good, not even in those days, so I wonder what they expected in return for money? Maybe labour, or some commitment for future earnings, perhaps.'

'Or worse?'

Lizzie shuddered, 'Well I'm really hoping Ellen never encountered that. I want to go to the processing area now.' She continued pulling at Faith's arm. 'I want to sit down, worry about it, and see what happens next.'

They found themselves seats side by side on one of the hard wooden benches that skirted the walls. Sliding on headphones, they listened to the recordings of memories and the family recollections passed down.

'The wait was several hours, Liz. Sure you don't expect us to do that, now do you?'

'Nope. Say I've just collected my bag Faith, passed my medical and I'm hanging on to my label and number.'

'Well done, girl. I think you are number thirteen on the manifest, shouldn't be much longer. Hope you don't need the toilet.'

Lizzie looked around the cavernous registration hall. 'What kind of toilet facilities would have been provided for the hundreds of waiting individuals and their wee ones, d'you reckon?'

'I am listening to this testimony now Liz, if you don't mind. It's all very upsetting. People who owe their fare to family back home, people being separated, one being allowed in and one not. What to do then?'

Faith's eyes had filled with tears, and her voice croaked.

Lizzie squeezed her hand. 'Shall we go down to the record department after they have done us, Faith? See what more there is to learn?'

Pulling her headphones off, Faith fumbled in her coat pocket for a handkerchief.

'Look, don't mock me. I know we aren't really being done. We are so much the lucky ones. Our Ellen would have sat here and heard languages she'd never heard before, probably hadn't even known existed. And coming from all over Europe, and further afield – Russia, Poland…'

'Poland is Europe.'

'Well it wasn't then. Or Czechoslovakia, which was Bohemia, Moravia, and Slovakia. Those would have been completely unknown.'

'Foreign even, you mean, Faith?'

'Yes, there wasn't a Czech republic until…'

'OK Faith, for a while there I thought you'd left your teacher hat behind. Come back, sister!'

'I'm back. Just musing. Did you see in the baggage hall, someone had brought a Singer sewing machine? That must have been a struggle, they weigh a ton.'

'Yup. I think struggle just about sums it up Faith. You've definitely caught the flavour of this place.'

They sat for a few moments longer, then Lizzie decided their number had been called.

Together they approached the doors which would offer freedom. Guarding the doors were tall mahogany desks and looking around, Lizzie imagined the room being full of hopefuls, carrying suitcases. She knew, from the photographs, that they would have been formally dressed. The men in suits and caps, women wearing neat long skirts and elegant in wide-brimmed hats.

She'd seen the elaborate national costumes. Women with babies in slings across their bodies; men toting bulging bags. Tired and queuing, they all lined up, hopeful but unsmiling. The children hungry, irritable, confused.

A ledger on the desk was simple and she peered closely at the neat columns of detail. Each column detailing name, destination, age, where from, who paid for ticket, amount of money carried. 'So this is the ultimate stage, Faith the last hurdle. Maybe it wasn't so very threatening.'

Turning to her sister, she exclaimed, clapping her hands together and doing a small jig. 'I'm in, but they want to ask you more questions!'

'OK. I'm up for that. What do they want to know, Liz?'

'Will you look after your sister if she falls on hard times?'

'I will.'

'Will you lend her money if she needs it?'

'I won't, but I will buy her a drink when we get to New York.'

'OK, you're in too!'

They grinned at each other, eyes meeting, not speaking. Lizzie leaned across the high desk front and planted a kiss on her sister's cheek.

'Welcome to America.'

Chapter 15

Ellen. New York: November 1906.

Noises she didn't recognise confused her and smells reminiscent of stale dishcloths smacked her face. After six days at sea, her senses had attuned to the sounds she needed. The signal for meals, a deep mournful gong, had been first to become familiar, then there were the sharp, urgent emergency drills. At night a lonely foghorn had penetrated her sleep. It comforted her, signalling that she was not alone. All smells when on deck were wind and sea. She expected she had become nose blind to the human scent in the washrooms and dining hall. Passenger companions crammed together, more in number than she had ever known. Some less washed than others.

Her nose twitched, trying not to inhale, as the dockside drew close. Oil, engines, dusty gravel and stale seaweed only slightly dampened the excitement of reaching dry land. Ellen turned her head oceanward, forcing her hands deep into her pockets. She would not smother her nose with a handkerchief.

'Move along, ma'am. We need to get off and processed before five o'clock. Don't want an overnighter here now, do ye?'

She'd been standing for a while at the side of the *Caronia*'s gangplank. Families weighed down with children, baggage and various family valuables were forming a line at the bottom of the steps.

As Ellen moved along the gangplank, she wasn't sure her usually steady feet would remember how to navigate the narrow quivering pathway. Joining the back of the queue she followed her fellow passengers into the imposing reception hall of the building.

Processing, that's what she understood it to be called, took several hours. There was good reason to not linger at disembarkation.

She'd hugged Bessie's bony frame before leaving for the tender, thanking her for the loan of the wide-brimmed hat. Gerald had been impressed when the historical photographer had chosen Ellen amongst a few other women passengers for a portrait. They needed one of 'Irish woman servant' and Bessie loaned her hat.

Ellen wished them both good luck with their futures. She thought it unlikely they'd ever meet again, but gave them Uncle Corrie's address 'just in case.'

Out the other side, she stood blinking in the daylight. Ellen, approved as an immigrant, joined the other successful passengers at the quayside. Everyone was jostling to get near the front, trying to see and be seen by men holding placards and notices, advertising jobs.

It reminded her of markets and fairs she'd visited in West Cork. Here the purchasers were agents needing labour. The vendors, immigrants with skills to sell, had choices. It was easy for her to get to the front. Unencumbered with bulky possessions and being tall and strong, she hoped she would soon find a job. She smiled and her shoulders relaxed when she read the offers.

Screwing her eyes, she was dazzled by the number of agents. She'd been used to hearing 'Sure yer lucky to have a job, any job at all' and 'Hang on to it, you never know when it might be ending'. Always, the same message. It would only take a poor harvest or an evil landlord or, in her case, a child, to cause the job along with the wages to disappear.

Here there were men offering futures. Raised arms, holding up placards reading "labourer wanted", "servant wanted." She watched for a while, as people approached the men. She wanted to see how they responded. Ellen liked the look of one man in particular.

He was a middle sized man of middling looks, and she noticed he'd taken care over his appearance. His grey felt fedora was set well back on his head like a watchful bird. His shoes were shining, jacket and trousers matched and seemed to be a fair fit. They didn't look, like many around him, as though they had been borrowed. A few appeared to be roughly put together, being worn out and ill fitting.

She liked the look of his face too. It was neither handsome nor plain, not finely chiselled nor plump, and his healthy complexion, she reckoned, made him no stranger to fresh air. His eyes were also unremarkable although they were unflinching, seeming honest and, viewed through thick spectacle glass, did not appear to be either narrow or mean. It was his kindly attitude which set him apart from the others.

She watched as he listened, head on one side like he was hearing poetry for the first time, to a woman with three children who approached him. His fresh air face clouded as she finished her conversation and he gently shook his head. Then he pointed her towards another couple of men with signs standing a few feet away.

Encouraged, she moved forward to read his sign.

'Young single woman good at reading and writing in English. Must be willing to help with children and general household requirements. Full board and lodging provided.'

Although there were other people all around, it wasn't long before she saw him look in her direction. She responded with a faint smile and a modest step forward.

'Name your skills ma'am, if you please.'

'I'm used to working to the gentry so I am and I finished National School with good grades.' Ellen hoped he wouldn't ask about arithmetic. Then she moved on with more confidence.

'I'm well used to looking after young children too. Indeed I can understand their likes and dislikes. I would keep them clean and safe too, although ye' do need to be watchin' them every moment.'

It seemed to Ellen that a long moment passed before she heard his response. She reckoned he was processing the information she'd just given him and perhaps he wasn't a man to make a decision in a hurry. Then his face broke into a smile and she ventured to introduce herself.

'I'm Ellen Clancey, by the way.'

Nodding and smiling, as though he'd heard of her already, he held out his hand and lowered his placard. 'Ma'am, I'm going to take you right along now to the mistress of the house. If she approves you will start tomorrow. If she doesn't approve, you'll have to come back here and take what's left over.'

Ellen, lifting her suitcase, hoped this would be the start of her new life.

'Well, that's fine, mister, but I won't come back to the dockside. I've an uncle here in New York is expecting me, so yes I'll go along with you now. An' if the woman doesn't want me will someone help me get over to his address? I don't want to be wandering around a big city alone the whole evenin' so I don't.'

Introducing himself as Mr Clark, Employment Agent, the ordinary-looking man raised an eyebrow at this request, which didn't alter his smiling friendly expression.

'Ma'am, I wouldn't let you do that. I'd accompany you myself. It would be an honour.'

Ellen hadn't expected this generosity but she agreed. Hardly believing the speed at which events were unfolding, she pinched herself and followed him as he strode away from the quay.

'This is Castel Garden.'

'Well isn't it just lovely?'

'You'll have heard of this famous concert hall, closed now, of course. But Jenny Lind sang here. Now it is the New York Aquarium.'

'Ah yes of course I've heard of Jenny Lind. An' I'm sure she went down well in the aqua-room.'

She couldn't prevent her eyes from widening at the size of the fortress. She promised herself that once she was settled, she'd come back and explore further.

'An' they're planning to build a Customs House here, need it to capture the taxes of all the imports. About time too.'

This was more familiar. She'd heard plenty of tales about evictions and families brought to the brink of starvation through taxes. 'An' if they can't pay their taxes what do you do ter them poor souls?'

'Taxes on imports, ma'am, not on the poor souls. Taxes on the rich souls. The ship owners and the merchants and the like.'

She sniffed noisily. She didn't believe that. She'd always known the poor were the first to lose out when rich people were asked for payment. She didn't expect New York would be any different.

'We're coming up to the start of Broadway now, ma'am, lower Manhattan to be exact. But I guess you know that.'

Ellen nodded, growing more confident of her responses.

'Now this here's called the Washington Building or sometimes the International Mercantile Marine Company.'

'I'm just lookin' at the signs there above the doors, Mr Clark. Says first class and cabin class, what's that for if you could tell me?'

'Selling steamship tickets for those going the other way, ma'am. You won't be going in there, I'm sure.'

Ellen stood for a moment, she needed to memorise the location of the pale grey stone building which stood in front of her, blocking the light. "Just along from the Battery Quay and at the foot of what he calls Broadway." Silently she promised her daughter, "I'll be back here for my ticket soon as I can. I'll be back for you, Cathy."

The walk up Broadway through lower Manhattan and past what he told her was the meat district, felt longer than the twenty minutes she'd been promised. Tall and tightly packed together, the buildings were different from anything she'd ever seen before. She was losing enthusiasm. Ellen stopped for a minute, putting her suitcase down and rubbing her shoulder.

Mr Clark's brow furrowed, his lower lip trembled, and Ellen realised he was a younger, less imposing man than she'd assumed.

'Miss Clancey, let me take your suitcase. I do apologise. You've had a long day I'm sure. I should have been more considerate, like.'

Ellie raised her eyebrows, astonished. She couldn't recall anyone helping her with anything she was carrying before. It didn't matter whether it was a basket load of laundry or a suitcase to New York. The noise and hard sidewalks combined with the distance they were travelling persuaded her. She passed the battered suitcase to Mr Clark, and watched him lift it onto his shoulder as though it were a bag of feathers.

Ten minutes later they entered a tree-lined square off upper Broadway. Four-storey red brick houses stood elegantly but bodyclose to their neighbours. Ellen was struck by their air of independence. These were not like the big house in Lahana, confidently dominating. They reminded her of the ornate Georgian three or four-storey buildings which bordered one side of the Annesley Bridge in Cork city. The whole square was quiet, seeming to breathe an air of security.

'These houses look smart,' she muttered, trying to tidy her hair. The trailing bun wouldn't, she felt, look refined enough for someone who might be employed here. She wished she'd kept Bessie's hat.

They stopped in front of a house which was built with the type of red brown brick she'd not seen before. It was draped in ivy, exposing tantalising glimpses of a wrought iron balcony. There was a gleam of upper-storey windows, familiar to servants.

Ellen squinted at the small windows below the eaves. That would be where she'd sleep, she supposed, and she wondered what it would feel like to share a bed with a stranger.

While she was assessing the building, Mr Clark climbed the steps and rang the doorbell, leaving her suitcase on the bottom step. Before Ellen had time to lift it the door opened and a stout black woman, in navy dress and white apron, nodded their admission.

Stepping inside the house she was disorientated by its tranquillity. She'd never experienced such silence, such a sense of waiting for a story to begin. Looking around, seeing more possessions than she imagined any one family could need.

'My employers at Lahana House were grand,' she shook her head in disbelief as she turned to Mr Clark. 'but they never had bicycles, coats, boots, umbrellas and mirrors in such numbers. I've never seen the like. Is this how they live in New York, the families?'

'The Rochesters do come from old money, Miss Clancey. Their history goes way back. Not everyone lives like this.'

'Do you, Mr Clark?' Ellen heard herself ask, knowing it was too personal a question. It was one which might scratch and not be wanted.

His expression tensed and it took him a moment before he replied, the smile fading.

'No, ma'am. I live simple.'

Ellen saw child-sized gumboots sitting alongside a teddy bear which appeared to have been discarded without any sense of order. The hallway was narrow, overfilled by two bicycles and a coat rack stuffed with clothing. The possessions emitted an air of hopefulness, waiting to be reinstated. Neither she nor Mr Clark spoke again, their silence adding suspense to the wait.

A clock on the wall, its pendulum producing a soft click at each swing, seemed to say 'wait and see, wait and see.' Ellen moved her weight from foot to foot. She wondered whether she might dare to lean against the curved oak bannister. After a few minutes she heard light running feet, soft enough to be unshod, descending the stairs.

A small, wiry-haired woman, her clothes a variety of mismatched colours, which somehow made her overall impression matched, landed at the foot of the stairs.

'Mr Clark, I thought you were never coming. Did you walk all the way? You could have got a cab. You know I'd have covered it.'

The agent shook his head. 'Wouldn't have troubled you, madam. We've had a pleasant walk through the town and this is Miss Ellen Clancey. I'm sure she enjoyed seeing all the sights along the way.'

Ellen shifted onto her heels and thought that a cab would have been a great idea. Her toes felt as if they were on fire and she ached with tiredness.

The small woman spoke cheerfully and with some surprise, as if she'd just received a bunch of flowers.

'Did I hear correctly, it's a Miss Helen is it? I'm Mrs Margaret Rochester. You can call me Mrs Margaret.'

She stretched out her arm, but Ellen hadn't expected the greeting and was late in putting her arm forward, so the gesture fell short.

'Ellen, Madam.'

'Pleased to meet you, Ellen. You must be tired; it's a long way from Battery Quay, and with a suitcase.' Mrs Margaret gave her agent a slight frown.

'If you'd both like to come in here and take a seat, I'll ask for some tea while we discuss details. Do leave your coat here in the vestibule, Ellen. I hope you can find a spare hook.'

Mrs Margaret looked from Ellen to her agent, before remarking gaily, 'You too Mr. Clark. Pleased to see you've already taken off your hat. I do admire good manners. You are a real gentleman.'

Ellen's spirits began to lift. She left coat and suitcase behind, in the hall she now learned was called vestibule, and followed Mrs Margaret. The room was dominated by tall sash windows, overlooking the square. Ellen's eyes were drawn to the view – a small park and lime green leafy trees.

"The children could play there," she reckoned. "I'd take them in the mornings after lessons and before we eat dinner. I wonder what their names are, the little Americans? Will they think I talk funny?"

'Do come over here Ellen. Please, take a seat.'

She pointed to an armchair with sagging cushions which gave the impression of having been recently vacated. Ellen was surprised. She had never been invited to sit in the Lahana household and eased herself, bottom first, dress smoothed behind her calves, into the seat.

Tea arrived on a tray, brought in by the same maid who'd opened the door. Dark-skinned and plump, she was a contrast to Hannah and Rose, the only other maids Ellen had known. Tight curls pulled back from her shiny wide boned face. These were held in place with a white cotton wrap. 'Thank you, Mercy. We'll be fine to serve ourselves here.'

Ellen liked the way Mrs Margaret spoke to Mercy. She wriggled further into the cushions, hoping being snuggled would secure her a place.

The interview took no longer than two cups of tea and several biscuits.

As Mr Clark got up to leave saying, 'I'll see myself out, thank you for the tea,' Ellen realised she had been hired.

He nodded, tipping forward the hat he was still holding 'Good luck to you, Miss Clancey, I'm sure you will settle in very well here.' She returned his nod as the first person she'd met in New York walked away.

Chapter 16

Ellen. New York: November 1906.

Mrs Margaret's pronounced drawl sounded, to Ellen, as though the woman was apologising. She described a plethora of small details. 'Always loses her hair ribbon' or 'I believe a son must have a sport,' she said. Flitting back and forth between topics like a nesting bird.

Trying to concentrate, Ellen forced herself to sit upright and look attentive. The accent was difficult to follow and the day had been chock full of unusual experiences. Her brain slowed. She pinched herself to keep alert.

Yes, sure, she knew she'd help the children, Maisie and Rob Junior, with their lessons in the afternoon, once she had walked them back from school. Well of course, if there isn't any livestock to look after and if Mercy was doing all the meals and clearing up work, what else would she do occasionally but run errands for Mrs Margaret? No, it wasn't at all too much to ask that she made sure the children's clothes and their rooms were clean and neat.

Ellen gazed around the room, 'the parlour' she'd been told it was. Mrs Margaret continued talking and she wondered how the Rochesters imagined this was normal. Rich with possessions and photographs; they certainly had money to spare. Several photographs hung from the walls, brown and lacy in faded frames. There were baby photographs and little children with long petticoats. And Ellen saw a younger version of Mrs Margaret, with a tall, serious looking man, both formally dressed, wearing hats.

Mrs Margaret had stopped speaking, waiting for a response.

'And in the morning, ma'am, after I've walked back from the school, and tidied up, and if you have errands, would you be wanting me to buy groceries?'

'I haven't decided on that yet Ellen, let's see how you get on with the children first. Perhaps we should see how long it takes you to keep the place tidy. Children can make quite a mess.'

Ellen nodded, flushed by the mild rebuke, turning her attention back to the room. First it was the puppets, Punch and Judy. They were familiar. She'd seen them in the shop in Skibbereen and been tempted to buy one for Cathy, but couldn't bring herself to spend the money. The gaudily painted wooden figures hung from a hook beneath the bookshelf, their stick-like limbs waiting to be brought to life. Over by the window a rocking horse on a sledge was caught mid-prance, its teeth gleaming white and the body decorated with flowers. Everything held a promise of children tumbling in, ready for play.

There were several samplers along one wall, their delicate cross stitching and pastel colours seemed detailed and perfect. They contrasted with the expectation of the toys. It was the small simple sampler, depicting a family of ducks which drew her attention. Pulling herself out of the deep seated chair she gave a questioning gesture to her new mistress, and crossed the room for a closer look.

'That one, MR. That was done by Maisie last year. It took her all year too, she's such a fidget.'

'Well done, little girl. I look forward to meeting you, so I do.'

She smiled and turned back to the centre of the room. Her eyes and limbs felt heavy. It felt like a lifetime since she'd left the tender. This was her new beginning, hers and Cathy's together.

'The children must meet you, Ellen. I will call you Ellen but they must address you as Miss Ellen. They won't settle tonight if they don't know who is going to help them get ready for school in the morning. Perhaps you could bear to wait a little longer before retiring?'

Mrs Margaret's long American vowels made the pronouncement of her name unfamiliar, so different from the short vowel used back home. Hearing it brought her back to the present. She nodded, feeling that her head might fall off. Bleary-eyed, she tried to focus.

Mrs Margaret pressed an ivory button on the wall and Ellen, hearing a bell ring further into the house, wondered whether the maid would have far to come. It used to take several minutes at Lahana House, but Mercy's response was almost immediate.

Ellen looked curiously at the stout black woman. She'd brought her farthing a week into school when she was a child 'for the black babies.' She had learned of savages living in huts being converted to Catholicism by their donations. That was all she'd ever heard. Except stories about pirates and slavery. And she'd seen a few black youths pushing carts or wearing advertising boards on her journey through Manhattan. Ellen braced herself for another unknown, reckoning it was likely she would share a bedroom with Mercy. 'Mercy please could you show Ellen here to her room, she'll want to unpack. Then, say give yourself a half hour to freshen up, Ellen, and I'll meet you down here at six o'clock. I'll have the children with me.'

Ellen heaved herself up once more, gathering her coat and suitcase from the hallway, wondering how she would know when it was six o'clock.

'Y'all follow me, Miss Helen.' The maid's longer softer drawl sounded unlike that of her mistress. Although the language was the same, she felt confused. The tongues so different from those she was used to. Hoping for a friend, she didn't correct Mercy on the pronunciation of her name.

Ellen followed Mercy a few steps behind telling herself that this was now where her old life ended and the new one began. The three flights of narrow stairs were navigated in a comfortable silence.

'Here y'are missy, your room. I'm across the way here and we share the washroom. They don't allow visitors. Did she tell you that? But honey, come an' go as you please. An' be in by ten o'clock, they bolt the doors here.'

Her round shining face beamed and her eyes widened, as though imparting surprising news. 'It's New York, honey, things are different here.'

Ellen threw herself onto the narrow bed, closed her eyes and tried to clear her head. She felt optimistic about living with the family. They seemed relaxed and kind.

Her cheeks flushed as she recalled asking Mrs Margaret about the shopping. 'Of course,' she chided herself aloud, 'I should have guessed they'd need to be sure I was trustworthy before allowing me to spend their money. Looking after children was a safe bet, no one would be likely to steal them. Money now, well that's a different matter.'

She'd been told by Gerard and Bessie to be wary around them. Americans didn't always say it as it was. Sometimes they boasted and bragged, they didn't like to tell people things which were difficult. She'd have to watch out for that, think her way through.

She sighed and rolled to the edge the bed. Pulling off her boots, she rubbed her toes through the thick woollen stockings. She had another pair of shoes, a lighter pair, lying in the top of her suitcase.

Slipping them on, she took her wash bag and crossed the hallway to the shared bathroom. Its white tiled surface gleamed and other than a petticoat hanging from the rigged-up line across the bath, there was no sign of use. Breathing in the strong carbolic scent of eucalyptus soap, her nostrils flared. She hummed as she unpacked her few toiletries and scrubbed her face and hands. Refreshed and less self-conscious about her stale appearance, she went back downstairs, following the sound of children's voices.

Ellen stood at the parlour door watching for a moment while two children jumped back and forth over a small stuffed toy lion. Mrs Margaret was seated by the window with some tapestry work on her knee, ignoring the children's activity. The little girl, Maisie, had a mass of blond curls, which stuck out on both sides of her head. It reminded Ellen of posters she had seen in the agent's store in Skibbereen, advertising the perfect American family. Maisie's pink, full skirted dress flounced as she jumped and she squealed every time her feet returned to the carpet. Ellen sighed quietly, recognising an attention-seeking child, a girl who'd soak up her attention and always look for more. She shuddered at the fancy pink frills, thinking they would have looked better on top of a fancy birthday cake than harnessed around a lively little girl.

'Maisie is, of course, the one making all the noise, and this is her younger brother Rob Junior. But we call him Junior,' Mrs Margaret explained, reaching forward, while staying in her chair. 'Our little son and heir. Such a good boy.'

Pulling him away from the game, she gave his hair a stroke with her hand, her face softening as she spoke.

'Now children, say "Hello, pleased to meet you Miss Ellen." Mercy will give you your supper tonight and you can see Miss Ellen in the morning, at breakfast.'

Their singsong voices repeated their mother's instruction and Ellen, pleased to realise that a child's voice crossed continents, enjoyed meeting them. She was disappointed to see them leave and looked forward to getting to know them better.

'If you'd like some supper before you retire Ellen, Mercy will give it to you in the kitchen once the children are finished. But you are free to go now, so I'll see you in the morning. My husband will be home soon, and I need to change for dinner.'

Ellen decided that sleep was more pressing than food. She

had eaten biscuits with tea only a couple of hours earlier, and for now she longed to be alone.

Over the following weeks, she found her life with the Rochesters very different from her previous experience as a servant in Ireland. There was no hard labour; she wasn't expected to lug laundry over fields, only to wash the children's clothes. On the other hand, she never knew when her work was finished.

She enjoyed the children, who were boisterous and inattentive, but there was very little free time in her working day. There always seemed to be some slight task or additional request. She called them the "Please could you just" requests. Before the end of the first week, Mrs Margaret had given her the responsibility of a small purse and a groceries list. Life was beginning to unfold. This was as good as she could have hoped it to be.

Mr Clark travelled "over from New Jersey" to visit one Sunday and asked to take her walking in Central Park. Before long he'd become a regular, insisting she call him George, and she found him to be interesting and fun. He had a store of magic tricks which he practiced on her. There were card tricks and other small illusions which she knew would have thrilled Cathy.

They visited the Metropolitan Museum, the lake at Central Park and the menagerie. He knew about wildlife. She squealed with delight when he pointed out the black squirrels, scampering across the paths, tame and curious. And he made her happy when he told her how she would love the acres of red and gold leafed autumn trees the following year. The acreage and winding pathways of Central Park were nothing like the landscape of West Cork, but to walk there relieved her spirits which sometimes felt clogged by the city.

Months passed. She wrote home every few weeks and only when she sent money the first Christmas did receive a brief reply. On the second Christmas she sent a separate package to Cathy, a winter coat in fine purple wool and a muffler edged in white fluffy rabbit fur, to hang around her neck. She'd never seen such style before and could imagine how pretty her little girl would look. She had to swallow hard when she realised that now she didn't even know the child's size.

The following March she received an unexpected letter. She recognised Michael's handwriting as soon as Mrs Margaret handed it to her after the children had gone for their evening tea.

Climbing the stairs, tripping but not quite running, she pushed open her bedroom door and ripped the envelope, using her teeth. Propping herself up against the iron bedhead and settling back on the bolster, she couldn't wait. News from home, such a treat.

She relished the privacy of having her own room. She'd adjusted the furniture, moving the foot of her bed below the window so she could see the sky. It was a narrow room, with a low ceiling and, being at the top of the house, it was hot and stuffy in the summer.

She liked the Rochesters. They gave her a day off every week and paid her well. 'That's for your services Ellen, we thank you.' A regular brown envelope of dollar bills on a Friday night. The family were kind but the relationship was professional. Sometimes they called her Helen, it seemed easier on the American tongue and she liked to think that was her American name. Although she didn't have to share a room or a bed she knew she couldn't bring Cathy here. No one knew about the child, although there were times with George Clark when she'd considered telling him.

Scanning the letter first, then reading it more carefully, her thoughts raced, taking in the possibilities which might now be on offer. She lay back and closed her eyes, leaving the letter on the bed, wanting to give herself more time to digest the contents.

Gurgling water sounds were coming from different parts of the house. They seemed to originate from the plumbing which ran behind her bedhead. She could tell that the family were washing up before their evening meal. She knelt on the bed, looking out the window at what Mrs Margaret called 'the yard'. It was small but laden with plants which thrive in shelter, most of which were unknown to Ellen before she came to America.

A high red-brown brick wall backed onto the house on the corner and edged the garden. In summer, heaps of creamy jasmine and woody trails of clematis had whispered across each other over softly dripping bunches of wisteria. Sometimes Ellen encouraged the children to scramble beneath their crumbling arches. Now the flowers were gone and she could see the bird feeders. The first time she noticed them was a surprise, she'd never thought it would be necessary to feed wild birds. In summer, she'd watch the sunset red Virginia creeper catch the evening light and almost become one with the old russet coloured wall. She often whiled away a half-hour just looking out her window at the wall and wondering whether the same sun was shining in Derryleague as in New York.

'Well, I sorted out the time in this house anyway,' she'd reminded herself. 'Sure I only have to listen to that ol' Dover wall clock, chimin' every hour day or night in America. What is it in Derryleague though? I know George told me how to work it out, but I really can't recall.'

Turning away from the window, she lifted the letter on the bed and read it again.

Dear Sissie,

I'm writing with news and I hope you are well.

We all miss you Sissie, you know that and you mustn't trouble yourself worrying over little Cathy. She is well used to you being away now. Calls our Mam 'Mammy' just like the rest of us, and she's started at the school.

We're all well enough here. Jim is still working in Dunmanway, in a draper's shop. You were here when he left us to get on with the farming, never was much of a farmer anyway. They expected him back though, but that hasn't happened. I think you getting involved with the decision to keep him at school caused a bit of a break-up between him and Dada, they needed the money, but you didn't agree about that. Anyway, Dada never really felt right about him so it was as well he went. But sure all that is old news. Here is my news. Mary Anne has left service and is getting married to Tommy O'Shea. Tis a pity you won't be at the wedding, it will be a grand do altogether. Will you write to her like, maybe send something?

And there was a bit of wailing going on up at the big house last month, the missus there, Lady Berish, she upped and died. Sudden like, never enquired what caused it but she had a grand funeral altogether and we had plenty of work setting out the tea and all. That son of hers is a right clown, his soul's gone to the devil they say. Well, him and his wife was there, she's the one with the money and needs keep him short. He's still at the gambling tables I hear, but he's older and lazy and fat as far as I can see. Has two little girls now, well younger than Cathy and not near as bright I'd say. Dressed to the nines in the black get up, hanging onto their mother. Anyway, thought you'd be interested. And that Hannah one, she's married too and funny thing was she was called back to help serve teas and of course I was there making sure those grand carriages were stabled and the lads looked after. And the automobiles, you couldn't believe them. That'd be the Linehans' money. Anyway, Hannah came up to me right after the funeral, before they all got back and asked did I know where you were living. I said nothing but asked her where she was living, said you might like to call in with her if it wasn't too far away. I think most people do know by now that you have gone but we've never given any details.

She said she was going to Kerry where her husband's family are from and I said I'd pass it on.

Now Sissie, I want you to know we are fine here and I know everyone expects an American relative, sure that's what I'll call you now, to send money back for fare and tis good you do so at Christmas. But there's no one here needs it, maybe just a small offering for Mary Anne. Just make sure you are set up yourself now and what it was that troubled you is far away.

We won't forget you, Sissie.

God Bless

Your brother Michael

Folding it carefully, she returned it to the torn envelope she'd so eagerly ripped and tucked it under her pillow.

She still had just over twenty pounds left from what she thought of as Lady Berish's payment. That was in addition to the dollar bills she had saved in a drawer underneath her petticoats. She knew she had more than enough to get her home and then return with Cathy.

Jumping off the bed and hugging herself with a grip as strong as her desire to act, she asked the room, already knowing the answer. 'Now shall I get a steamship ticket tomorrow or should I wait a bit?'

Chapter 17

Ellen. West Cork: June 1908.

Pushing one foot in front of the other, Ellen shuffled down the gangplank. She was wedged in the middle of the queue, the suitcase bumping against her legs. Her heart was swooping and sinking between anticipation and disappointment as she searched the quayside for a familiar face amongst the home crowd.

"Well thanks Michael, you got my letter I'm sure, no bother to reply. Not important is it, me coming back?" Stepping off the gangplank she made her way through, thinking about the length of time since she'd heard of Lady Berish's death.

"Three months ago I got the letter and another couple I reckon, before I heard from ye that the woman who was the cause of my leaving is dead. That's now five or six months. And Hannah gone too. Safe now, I'm safe now"

'Move along now, please. No loiterin' on the quayside, there's ones wantin' to come aboard.'

She smiled, her ears warming to the Irish accent. How she had missed it. "Such a relief not having to think hard on every sentence. An' sure I'm home," she thought, as she walked down the gangplank. "This feels familiar now, so different from last time." A shiver of the heartbreak memory crossed her mind. "An' Cathy? I wonder, have ye grown much in the past eighteen months? I'm not even thinking about would ye have grown away from me now." Ellen shook her head, hoping to dislodge the idea. It was a persistent fearful whisper, asking to be considered.

"Well now, I hope these lovely American style clothes I'm

bringing will help her feel ready to start out on a new life with me."

She gave one last search across the waiting crowd. Some were waving to returning passengers, others holding children on shoulders. She pushed though, muttering an apology, edging her way into town and on to the station.

Settling into the women's carriage, she closed her eyes, recalling the events that had taken place since receiving Michael's letter. It had spurred her on to visit Uncle Corrie. Knowing she should have contacted him when she'd arrived, she couldn't go home without seeing him.

She had never given him the black pudding from Conakilty, instead she'd given it to Mercy to cook. The children had loved it. She did feel a bit guilty but persuaded herself that a two year old meat sausage wouldn't have done any favours to an old man's constitution.

It had taken her all her courage to step up to his door. She drew on the bravery she'd shown many years before stepping up to the door at Lahana House. She knew she could do it. She could beg for a bit of help, again.

A stooped figure, his hair grey and thinning met her at the door. Apart from his slightly jaunty moustache, his face was lined with a downward drift. He bore no resemblance to any of the men in Ellen's family and she wondered whether she had made a mistake with the address. 'Uncle Corrie? Is it Corrie Clancey? I'm Ellen Clancey. I wrote to you last year, come over from Queenstown on the sailing to New York. Did you get my letter?' His welcome was no warmer than Lady Berish's had been. 'Ah, it's yourself at last is it? Here more than a year and this is the first time you think to call on me.'

His shoulders crept up towards his neck and he pinched his lips into a tight blue line once he had finished speaking, as if to preserve his breath. He didn't ask Ellen why she hadn't been in contact and she didn't offer an excuse.

He indicated, with a nod, that they should move into a parlour. The room was shaded by lace curtains the same grey colour as his worn and baggy pullover. He waved a claw-like hand towards a hardback chair before shuffling out to make them both a cup of tea. Although he'd been critical, the old man hadn't seemed surprised by her visit and when he left the room Ellen had time to look around.

A layer of dust frosted every surface, she'd expected that, but she was surprised by the threadbare sofa beneath the window and the cracked linoleum flooring. The mantel above the unlaid fireplace displayed a square wooden clock which gave a gentle click as each minute passed. She concluded that the room, and probably the rest of the house, could do with a clean.

Corrie Clancey returned carrying a metal tray stained with circular brown tea rings. It held two cups and saucers and a plate with two biscuits. Ellen decided she shouldn't wait any longer.

'I've come to ask a favour, Uncle Corrie. I've a young daughter. Her father, my husband, has disappeared. 'And now,' she'd explained, putting an effort into making her voice sound confident, 'Now I need to bring her over. And we will need somewhere to stay.'

Sitting on the stiff parlour chair balancing a cup and saucer of tepid of tea in one hand, and a stale biscuit in the other, Ellen had held her breath.

Uncle Corrie, who had been in New York as long as he'd been in Ireland, didn't show a flicker of emotion in his pale narrow eyes. Ellen waited for his response, her optimism fading.

'You've a good position with those Americans, have you not? Is there no spare room in their big house? An' I've no space here, none at all. I'm a bachelor but I need these rooms let out, 'tis what I live on. I'm too old to go out shopkeepin' anymore, an' I've no one to look after me in the old age. Sure I need to be careful, you wouldn't expect the Yanks to look after me, would you now?'

Ellen released her breath, long and slow, through her nose, staying calm. The stiff brocade collar of her Sunday best outfit tightened around her neck as she attempted a weak smile.

'I need a room. Can't pay much, maybe something for the child, but I'll do your household chores for ye', cookin' an' the like. Wouldn't it be great for you to have someone of your own here? A nice bit of Irish baking, some potato bread, or wheaten scones maybe? Or a good stew in the evening, a bit of bacon. An' I can do laundry too. What do you say, Uncle? We'd be no trouble.'

His features remained impassive, seeming to be carved in stone. His pale eyes had sharpened and she noticed him biting his lower lip. The moustache quivered and eventually twitched as he broke the silence.

'I'll not say yes and I'll not say no. I've to think about what's best for myself now. What age is this child? I suppose you'll tell me she's sweet an' mannerly. All mothers say that in my experience. An' then the little beggars get under the feet and make a noise in the night, an' they're picky over their food. I seen it all in other houses. My men, my lodgers, I don't know how they'd take it.'

'Shall I come back tomorrow then, Uncle Corrie, give ye time ter consider?'

'Termorrer? Nah. I'll write. Wait 'til you hear from me then if it's a yes, come back an' we can make arrangements. I'm not puttin' myself out o'er it though, I can tell you that fer nothin', girl.'

'I thank you for yer time, I'm sure, Uncle.' Ellen replaced the half-eaten biscuit and unwanted cup of tea onto its grubby metal tray.

'I'll see meself out, so I will.'

Ellen stood up, her pride injured and her hopes diminished. As she turned she swished her ankle length serge skirt, a new purchase for the journey home, hoping the style couldn't go unnoticed.

'I'll be back,' she muttered to the shabby door, as she inched it closed behind her. The frame looked splintered and she certainly didn't want to be blamed for a crack. 'An' you need a lick o' paint, in more ways than one.'

Disappointed and struggling to prevent hot tears from overflowing, she walked the mile alongside Central Park back to the Rochesters' house on Broadway. Rounding the corner of the square, she saw the outline of a man dressed in a suit. She could see a starched shirt front under the jacket, its tie a flash of blue check giving the outfit a pop of colour.

George Clark was standing at the doorstep. She'd been flattered by his attention at first and now expected his visit on her days off. "That is just what I need" she thought. " A relaxing, undemanding companion, someone who likes to be with me, just for myself." She walked faster as she got closer. "I know the Rochesters are kind, but once I leave they'll forget me. I hope he doesn't."

'George, hello. Lovely surprise.' Wiping her eyes with her knuckle to clear her vision and straightening the brim of her hat, she switched on a smile.

'Oh Helen, must you always say that? I'm here every time you have a day off.' He took her hand and gently brushed her wrist, a feather duster of a movement. She froze, not wanting the moment to end. It was as close to a display of tenderness as she'd felt since she left home.

'Let's walk, shall we, George. Anywhere, I don't care where.'

Taking her arm, George began walking slowly down the street, in the direction he had come, back towards Central Park. She felt a rustle behind her ear and giggled when he pulled a small lace handkerchief out. 'Magic!' He announced, as though surprised himself. 'A small gift for a beautiful lady.' He handed it to her with a flourish, watching as she dabbed her eyes.

'Are you alright Helen? Ellie? You seem upset. I thought you were going to meet your uncle. How was he?'

'Helen's the American me, George, no Ellie today. And Helen, well, just make her laugh a bit will you, she needs a cheer up!'

Walking with him along Upper Broadway, turning onto their familiar pathway, a side entrance onto the park, Ellen's mood lifted. George was fun, with his magic tricks and his sense of adventure. She wondered whether he might bring a glimmer of a possibility, her options were running out.

Breaking his stride with no warning, right in the middle of the sidewalk, narrowly missing two young boys dragging a cart full of early evening newspapers, he asked, 'Would it surprise you to learn, Helen, that I have a child?'

Ellen was shocked. Her first thought was to wonder whether she'd been sharing her thoughts aloud, not sure how this might relate to Cathy.

'Well it would, yes.' Ellen looked up at him, her eyes widened, her eyebrows raised. There was no doubt about it, she was amazed that such an important part of his life had remained hidden. 'But it's a wonderful thing, a child. Where is the child?'

'He's at school, weekly boarding school, in New Jersey. I have him at weekends. That's when I do my magic tricks. Keeps him amused and brings his friends round to enjoy the entertainment too.'

'And his mother?'

'I thought you knew. I am a widower, Helen. Did Mrs Margaret never say? My wife passed away three years ago. I live alone now, and that's no life for a boy. He's coming ten year old. Can't live in a house with a man who's out all day at work. And by the way, isn't much of a cook.'

'I have to tell you similar, George. One which perhaps I should have mentioned earlier but it is a sore memory for me and I don't speak of it often.'

Her voice quivered, taking a deep breath before continuing.

'I have daughter, a sweet darling little girl. The image of her dear, dead papa. He was taken from me so suddenly. An overnight fever and in the morning he was gone. I left her behind in Ireland with my parents. They adore her but she is pining for me as I am for her and we need to be reunited.'

'Oh my dear, why did you not tell me this before?' George didn't seem discomforted by her news. Ellen wondered whether he had suspected there was a mystery in her past.

'You must be heartbroken, poor brave lady. To go from wife and mother to daily help, well nanny anyway.' He flushed, correcting himself stumbling over his words, hoping to bypass the slight. 'In a foreign country,' he continued, when Ellen didn't respond. 'Far away from those who love you and look out for you. And the poor dear child. Of course you must be reunited without delay.'

'But how can I, George? I can go back to Ireland and never return to New York or I can stay here and pine the rest of my life for my baby and never know a day's happiness again.'

'Is there not a third way, Helen? Could not the child come here?'

Ellen's words were slow and deliberate, sounding wretched. There could be no misunderstanding, nothing to obscure the drama she was playing out. She found herself thinking she was on a doorstep again, needing help.

'That has always been my dream, George. But I can't afford a place of my own. The Rochesters won't have her, my uncle won't have her. No. I fear there is nothing for it but for me to return to Ireland as soon as I have arranged my steamship fare.'

George didn't speak, and twisted his fedora nervously between his hands, before slapping it on his head. He pulled her towards him, steered by his grip on her elbow.

'My home is big enough for us to share. I've rooms in a house in New Jersey. They are yours if you would say the word.'

This was exactly where Ellen had hoped the conversation might go. 'And what word would that be George? What could you possibly want from me?'

'Your hand, Irish Ellie and American Helen. Make me the happiest man in New York and marry me.'

'That's two hands, George.' Ellen replied, laughing. 'You are too good. A real saviour so you are. Y'know ever since we met at Battery Quay, I knew you were someone I could depend on.'

She remembered how miffed she'd felt about the unordered cab, but now she thought his frugal approach to money was just what she needed. She considered herself careful too, hating to see money wasted.

She bent her head then, before replying, wanting to appear coy and flushed. She had recently been reading "Little Women" and decided that was how young American women behave in situations that call for modesty.

'Why, I thank ye, George. Sure I'd be delighted to marry you.'

'So how will we see about your child, Helen?'

'I'll go back to Ireland first, collect my Cathy. Then I can bring her back an' sure we can be a family, all four of us.'

Her effort to sound modest had turned out rather flatter than she'd intended. She thought it sounded more like the tone she'd use at the grocery store when checking her change. George didn't seem to mind and continued the conversation as they carried on with their walk.

'Of course, you must do that. I understand. When would you plan to make the journey?'

Ellen, having already booked a ticket to sail at the end of the month, overlooked that detail.

'I think I'll try and go at the end of the month. Summer in Ireland then back in autumn with Cathy so she can start school here.'

There had been little more said about her plans. George had bent over and lifted the net back from her hat brim, which was covering half of her face. She'd enjoyed the brush of his moustache against her lips. Relieved that her immediate future was secured, Ellen linked her arm in his, breathing in the masculine mixture of pipe smoke and damp wool.

And now, three weeks later, here she was back in Queenstown again. Ireland hadn't altered she reckoned, but she certainly had. After changing trains in Cork, she found herself a corner seat in the carriage, sleeping most of the way. She jolted awake as the train steamed and hissed into Derryleague station.

Stretching her cramped legs and shrugging on her coat, she levered open the carriage door before alighting, one hand on door, clutching her suitcase in the other. She found it difficult to keep her trailing skirts from catching on the metal edgings of the steps.

'Sissie. Hey girl, over here look ye! Smart lookin' ye are too.'

'Michael. Oh how great to see you Mikey. Thanks for coming to meet me.'

'Sure I met the train yesterday an' all Sissie. Wasn't sure when you were berthing. Didn't say on the papers only the departure.'

'Well, here I am and well pleased to be here too.'

'I'll take your case, Sissie. Full of gold, I'm sure!'

Ellen blushed, the suitcase was full of gifts for Cathy but hadn't included much for anyone else. There was a small gift for Jimmy and she reckoned she'd have to use a few dollars to give those at home a small package each. Well, she reasoned, she'd been careful with her wages, spending as little as possible and keeping her mind on Cathy's future. She expected that the proposal from George would now make her ends meet more comfortably.

'How's everyone?' Settling herself into the car behind Michael's horse she waited until he'd cracked the whip and given the horse the order to go. She needed his full attention, to be sure that what she read on his face was a response to her, not to the horse.

'Fine, all grand. I told ye Mary Anne married so there's a bit more room now. An' I'll be next, so I will. I'm goin' wi' Deirdre Regan an' she's real soft on me so she is. So there would be room for ye, Sissie, were ye to want ter stay.'

'Thanks Michael, but no. I'm going back in a couple of weeks or so, haven't booked it yet. I want to get things settled with Cathy. I've a place for her. We will have a home, a proper home. I'm to be married.'

Michael pulled the reins hard. The horse snorted and tossed his head before stopping at the edge of the road. Turning sideways in his driving seat, Michael's luminous brown Clancey eyes looked troubled.

'Now Ellen. Get this straight. Cathy is happy here. She's settled, she's enjoying school an' she's bright. Reading and writing English comin' along now and speaks English outside the house too, so she does. Dada and Mam are her Ma and Da now, just like they are to the rest of us. And although she is the youngest, she's fitted in just fine. They dote on her so they do, the old ones.'

Ellen frowned and shook her head, as though an insect had caught in her hair. She didn't want to hear about how Cathy was loved by the family. A jealousy-inspired bile filled the back of her throat and she couldn't speak.

Chapter 18

Ellen. West Cork: July 1908.

'Not now Ellen, not in front of the child.'

'Then when Mam? When can we agree? I've every right and I've made all the arrangements.'

Several times a day she'd asked, even during their first meal. She'd been determined they should know she intended to take Cathy back with her, but she'd been pushing against the tide of her parents' opinion.

They'd stood outside, by the stone wall, to welcome her back. Everyone waving and hugging all at once. It reminded Ellen of the farewells she had witnessed in Derryleague station when she left. No one had objected either, when she'd fussed over Cathy like a ewe reunited with a lost lamb. After the initial excitement, she'd had to turn her head away when she saw how Cathy followed Mam about. She didn't correct the child when she'd been greeted as Sissie.

Before the meal that first evening, small packages of dollars had been distributed amongst siblings. She had given a slightly fatter envelope to her father. 'For you and Mam. Buy something nice or maybe take her to Cork for the day.' His single raised eyebrow told Ellen all she needed to know about the destiny of those dollar bills. She'd bought a book describing, in exaggerated detail, the positive aspects of life in America. That was for Jimmy.

'For you Cathy, I've bought coloured socks, they made these in a factory in America. I didn't knit them myself and here's two pretty petticoats, all the little girls in America wear these.'

'Do all the little girls have bows in their hair, Sissie? Are they just like the posters at the Oifig an Phoist?'

'Well, lots of them are Cathy, but none as pretty as you. I can get bows for your hair, would you like that, darling?'

Her father cleared his throat and her mother clattered crockery irritably as she passed around the steaming dinner plates.

Ellen had promised not to mention her intentions to Cathy until she'd had time to get to know her better, but it was no use. As she tried to steer every conversation, it seemed magnetically drawn towards the compass which was her daughter.

'Now yer Da got one of his pigs slaughtered for the occasion, Ellie, an' it's been hanging' since Monday.'

'Say Grace, Dada.'

The echo of a rhythmic mumbled grace before meals smooched around the table and the family stilled for a few moments.

Once the prayer had ended 'trí Chríost ár dTiarna, Amen' there had been an impatient clatter of cutlery. Mam's encouragement "bí ag ithe anois, bí ag ithe" had raised Ellen's mood. She had missed using the Irish tongue and 'be eating now, be eating' was a superfluous encouragement. There was no talking. The family reaching across one another with filled mouths and dedicated chewing.

'Now this is a real American Homecoming,' Mam had announced, flushed by a mix of excitement, anxiety and oven heat.

As Mary Clancey leaned over steamig filled plates, Ellen noticed her mother, never a slim woman, had put on weight. She was pleased to think that this wasn't the only time the family enjoyed plenty.

'Mam, this would be better if we didn't have to talk about

America all the time.' Nora's squeaky voice broke the silence. Ellen had forgotten the thin petulant tone of her younger sister's voice. Nora was always trying to wriggle a wider space for herself within the tight family group. 'We got along fine without Sissie at Christmas.'

'Well, I missed you all every Christmas. The decorations in New York were lovely and bright and the electricity there is all over the place, they don't have to worry about the cost. And the Rochesters always included me in their family day, but I really felt lonely alright.'

'Well, sure maybe Sissie, you will stay home now and be with us next Christmas?'

'Mikey, you know I can't do that. I've a return ticket, and a job to go back to. I'm making a new life so I am…'

'Enough about Amerikay, girl. Let us tell ye' about Ireland.'

Her father rarely spoke when there was food on the table, so although they continued eating, it was as a secondary occupation and the family lifted their heads, giving an impression of paying attention.

'We've come up in the world, as they say, an' with the new tenant landlord agreements, we're better off than before. Having our own farm like and not being tied to the Berish family. They're nothing to us now, are they?' He swallowed and looked around the table, checking everyone was listening.

Ellen blushed, her father's implication unclear. "I know you know some of it Dada, but maybe not everything," she thought. He continued talking, not looking in her direction. 'Tho' they still lord it over us, an' we watch what we say. The uprising isn't over yet.'

Michael, Dan and Nora looked as though they had heard it before, and returned their attention to the plates.

'Sure Dublin was awful, so it was.' Michael interrupted, which allowed his father, with a nod to Mam, to indicate his need for another piece of meat. 'I didn't go anywhere near. An'

Cork had its riots too. While there was some around here got involved, we kep' our heads down.'

Ellen, ignoring Nora's frown, continued navigating her own conversation stream, distancing herself from Berishes or uprisings.

'The weather in New York is quite different to here Cathy and you'll need warm in winter and cool in summer. I'll buy you more, of course, when you grow out of what you've got.'

Cathy had looked at her in surprise. 'Will I be going to New York, Sissie? Will we all be going?'

While Ellen had to swallow hard every time Cathy called her Sissie, she couldn't hold back from her intentions. 'Sure Cathy, you're coming back with me. I've made arrangements for you. We have a lovely house to go to and I'll tell everyone all about it once we've had our supper now.'

'Mammy, am I going away?' As Cathy's small anxious face turned to her grandmother, Ellen's stomach felt a lead weight of disappointment settle. She couldn't swallow.

'No Cathy, you aren't going anywhere girl. You've your friends and your schoolin' an' this is your home.'

Ellen put her head in her hands as Cathy slid down from the table, making her way round to the older woman. The small child's body leaned against the solid bulk of her grandmother, as though confident of her protection. Ellen felt a vast distance, a sad, barren wasteland, between her and her child.

Over the next couple of days Ellen tried to rekindle the closeness she had had with Cathy, unable to believe that it had vanished so entirely.

Her mother didn't interfere with any plans she made for spending time with the child. As both women shared household chores, it gave them plenty of time to argue the options.

'You can come back here if you want, Ellen. We've more room now Mary Ann is away and Michael says he's going soon too. Jim works in Dunmanway, as you know, so it will only leave Dan, Nora, and Cathy here. Plenty of room for you, if it's what you want.'

'No Mam, it isn't what I want. I've not telled you yet, but I'm engaged to be married. George. He's a widower, an' he has a son. Older than Cathy, about ten I think. Anyway, he has his own house an' I'll be giving up my work with the Rochesters once I'm married and then Cathy can have a grand life altogether. She'll be living in New Jersey, going to school an' makin' new friends. Of course we will be back to visit, we won't lose touch.'

'Ellie, you're a wonder, so you are. The fare back from Amerikay is a man's wage, for a year, you'll not be coming back and fore easily. An' when you left you were running away from that hold Lady Berish had over ye. Well, now she's gone, so you can settle here again. Cathy's at school. You can get a job in town, in a shop maybe, and we can go back to the old way.'

'No, Mam. There can't be any going back, not now. I can't spend the rest of my life living here. Is it a spinster I'll be? Or an unfortunate woman with a child who everyone knows doesn't have a father. That's a bigger problem on Cathy than if I am away. 'Tis better for both of us to go back, make a new life.'

The arguments continued every day, often well into the evening. As far as possible, both women kept their raised voices and snapping tempers away from the child.

Ellen knew she'd have to book her departure within a couple of weeks, her ticket was only valid for a month. Lying beside Nora in the girls' room at night, she felt the weight of her decisions hanging over her.

Closing her eyes, she could see two towering funnels rising above the rooftops in Queenstown, beckoning, waiting and reproaching her for reluctance. She knew it wasn't a fanciful reproach; she needed to secure Cathy's place on the steamship with her as soon as possible. And she needed an ally.

'I'm going to see Jim today, Mam. In Dunmanway. I'll get the train. Can Michael or Dada take me to the station, if the horse car is free?'

'An' when you've talked this madness over with your brother, we can settle it tomorrow night. You can make your travel arrangements or cancel them, whichever you decide. But no more arguments now. Right, Ellie?'

Ellen nodded. She knew she could rely on Jim. The one she always thought of as her baby. Not any more, of course. Even her own baby wasn't a baby anymore. Jim would see her side of it, she was sure, and maybe he could help her persuade Dada and Mam. Although mostly it was Mam needed persuading.

⟞⟝

Entering the dimly lit draper's shop where Jim worked, the smell of worsted cloth and wool, rich and oily, made her nostrils search for more. On top of the polished wooden counter, a silver measuring strip embedded along one side, were reels of cotton: red, yellow, green and brown. The neatly stacked pyramid of reels were piled beside cards of buttons, inviting touch. Smells and sights distracted her and she paid little attention to the man in a white apron who was stacking the shelf at the back of the room. The motes of dust which danced across the few shards of light escaping between the heavy window curtains made his outline vague.

'Could I speak to James, please?'

As the thin, stooped figure turned towards her, she had a moment to compose her face before responding. 'Jim. I thought that was you, but I wasn't sure. You've not visited since I came home. Did you not know I was back? Dada says you have little free time so I'll excuse you, so I will. Come here and give me an American Homecoming hug.'

Twenty months had changed him. He had grown taller, but

his sparse frame looked like it was hung with damp washing. Perhaps, she thought, he hadn't thrived all that much away from home. His deep-set blue eyes, which glittered like moonlight on the night sea, were unchanged but his red hair had turned a sand dune tussle.

'Darling Jimmy. You're lookin' great so ye are.' She wouldn't mention the new lines on his face and although he smiled a warm welcome, there was something hesitant about his approach which was unsettling.

'Would you have any time for us today at all, Jim? I've been lookin' forward to seeing ye and hearin' how you're gettin' on.'

'Dinner break in half an hour, Sissie. I close the shop then until two. Meet you outside, on the square at one. I've a packet here. I usually eat it under the chestnut tree. We can share, so we can.'

'I'll buy something Jimmy, don't need to take your food from you. I'd have treated you to a hot dinner if you'd had time, but anyway we can meet outside, that's as good.'

Ellen left the shop, and, turning up Main Street, bought an apple and a bag of shortcake biscuits from the grocer shop. She'd become used to purchasing ready baked goods in America, but had never expected to do so in Ireland. She kept her face straight when told the price. Her mam would have made the biscuits for a fraction of the cost and she'd never paid for an apple.

Checking that they didn't mark the book she had brought for her brother, she wrapped the bag with her purchases into her scarf. Gathering her skirt in one hand, she pulled away from the shop door. The bell which was on a rusty and imbalanced spring had clanged an urgent warning as she'd entered. It was unpleasant and she didn't want to hear it again.

Ellen's boots tapped a sharp rhythm on the cobblestones of the road as she walked slowly up and down and around the square, killing time. The street was silent apart from the noise she was making and the discreet, unhurried air of the town soothed her. It was a pleasant contrast to the bustle of New York. She'd expected the quiet, and as she was unfamiliar with the town she decided to look around.

Dunmanway wasn't large, similar in size to Derryleague. A population of fifteen or sixteen hundred she'd heard tell. Only ten miles between the towns but she knew no one in the streets around the square.

She didn't have to crane her neck to see the top of the buildings, and recalled how astonished she'd been by the New York towers. It hadn't taken her long to get used to their heaven-scraping heights.

Without warning, a wave of homesickness threatened to put her off balance. Sitting down on the bench in front of the chestnut tree, she felt herself cast adrift from those places where she had a safe mooring. The house on the square, the figure of George Clark on the doorstep. Was it their distance or their familiarity, she wondered, which made her long to see them again?

Shuffling her scarf and bag around to give herself more space, she watched Jim emerging through the shop's door frame. He was hurrying out with an old metal lunch pail, which had the name Maguire painted on the outside. His eyes darted up and down the square before resting on her.

"Perhaps," she thought, "he didn't believe I'd be waiting. How could he think that? I'll always be there for Jim."

Smiling across at her, he locked the door, letting the closed sign swing in the window.

'Jim, is something the matter? You don't look very happy. An' you haven't visited at home, has there been a row or what?'

The rest of Jim's face didn't correspond with the half smile he offered. She wondered whether she saw pain, certainly she'd touched on something deep. Ellen waited, knowing he wasn't one for confrontations, and held her breath, not wanting to break the silence.

'I'm so miserable Sissie. Not sure they'll ever want me back in the house now. I'm no good on the farm an' they weren't happy about my schooling. I've you to thank for persuading them to let me finish. Anyway, I did finish. I had hoped, by now, to have bettered myself. But I'm stuck here an' I'll just have to get on with it.'

'So what's the problem? You were here before I went away and it was fine then. Can't you just visit?'

'It was alright at first, but they thought it was just a notion I had, y'know? I can't send money back to the farm, there isn't any spare, so that's a disappointment. They would expect a shilling or two now and again or better still have me work on the farm, but I'm not doing that. I'm a bit wasted, so I am. I think maybe they've forgot me.'

'An' what is it you really want to do? Never mind about them. Will you stay here or get work somewhere that might better yourself?'

'Sissie, y'know, I just don't see it. There's nothing around here I could do. Shop work is all I'm fit for. An office job would need connections or some training and sure we don't know anybody would help us get started now, do we?'

Considering the no longer fresh and unlined face of her younger brother, Ellen saw the toll this lonely existence was taking on him. She felt the book she'd bought him weighing heavily in her bag. Would it be an encouragement or make him more unsettled, she wondered.

The bench was too narrow for them both to set out their lunch so they moved to sit on the wall edging the square and unwrapped their food. Ellen laid several biscuits alongside James's mixture of overboiled potatoes and onions.

Putting her hand out to touch his arm, needing physical contact with the person she trusted most in the world, the words she which had been chocking her mouth tumbled out.

'Jim, I've a big problem with the family, so I have. They won't let me take Cathy back.'

171

'I know that Sissie, I knew that from the day you left. It was always going to be difficult. Once you left, they changed her name. You know that don't you?'

'Well, I suppose her name of Riley wasn't really legal. I never actually married Patrick Riley so it's fair enough to say she's Clancey. I'm not worried about her having the same name as me though, won't raise questions at immigration.'

'An' is it easy, like, to get in. Questions an' all?'

'You'd be amazed at the number of mistook names there is going in. I heard one man told he'd need to shorten his name to fit in better, so he just shrugged his shoulders. Poor tired man, he looked too, and agreed. Dropped the "stein" at the end of his name.'

Her brother nodded, his mouth full, his eyes never leaving her face.

'An' here's one you'll love, Jimmy boy. Well, it's a story was going round I heard while I was queuing up. So this Irish inspector asks an immigrant in the registry hall, "What's your name?" He's Jewish, doesn't speak much English, tired and worried too, I'm sure. Anyway, he mumbles some foreign words, something like "far gessen," so the Irish inspector says, "Ferguson then, right, on you go". So Ferguson is his name now. Can you believe it? And they nearly all call me Helen over there. I didn't like it at first but now I don't mind a bit. The American me is Helen and the real me, the Irish me is Ellen. Always Sissie to you though.'

James crammed one of her biscuits into his mouth, the sweet crumbs falling onto his shirt front. Ellen resisted the impulse to brush them off, as she would have done for Maisie or Rob Juniour.

'An' how is the American Helen doing these days?'

'Workin' and savin' to get her daughter back. That's all I see in my future, Jim. I've met a real good man. Name's George. George Clark. Widower with a son, little bit older than Cathy but she will have a step-brother and we will be a proper family.'

'But d'ye like it ? Amerikay I mean.'

'I like it well enough. It's very different, fast an' noisy but the people, you know, they're not so very different. Some are real nice and welcoming, some are arrogant and think they're too good for ye and there's plenty of poor people there too. It's not all gold and honey.'

They were silent for a moment. Ellen knew she couldn't express just how different New York felt. It wasn't a six day, one year's salary distance, it was the variety, the choices, the easy transport. All the things that people in America took for granted.

'I came over a bit funny just now, walkin' down the street there. I remembered my place in New York and I missed it.'

'Didn't expect that did you Sissie? Maybe you've been too soft with your memories.'

'It's just that it's not all that strange anymore an' you're not wrong, Jim, I might not be happy living back in West Cork. And if I can't live in West Cork then I'll go back to America. But not without Cathy.'

Leaning back, Ellen tipped her head to catch a hint of warmth from the weak sunshine and closed her eyes. George Clark, Mrs Margaret, Uncle Corrie, Mercy, the children. They swam across her vision, silhouettes behind her eyelids, seeming as close and real as her family.

'Can I take another biscuit?'

She opened her eyes and looked at him, nodding.

'Jimmy boy, if I make it in the States I'll send for you, so I will. There will always be a home for you wherever I am living. You know that, don't you?'

James munched his biscuit, more crumbs falling down the front of his shirt, before he licked his finger and dabbed them. When he looked up she thought his expression of anxiety lessened and a flicker crossed his eyes, which she wondered might be hope. Why, she chided herself, had she not thought more seriously about it before?

173

'Of course, Jim. That's what we'll do. Cathy and me. We'll go back, I'll marry George and once that's settled and we are in his house I'll send for you. I've a bit left over after I pay the fare back for Cathy, so I'll soon get yours, I promise. Sure I won't be payin' rent or anything, I can do some work and save a bit. You'll see, we will do it.'

She didn't know why the silence between them felt heavy, ominous. It reminded her of a storm waiting to break. But she knew with Jim there would never be more than a light rainfall between them.

'Ellen.' She widened her eyes, knowing this must be a serious conversation if he used her given name.

'Ellen. They're not going to let her go. You do know that, don't you?'

'No.' Her mouth dried, tears threatened to break the banks of the control she'd built and her hands clenched at the crumbly greaseproof paper bag in her lap.

'No. She's mine. She's my little girl, and she's coming with me.'

'D'ye ever wonder?' James stopped and bit his lip, suddenly looking away from her. 'D'ye ever wonder what Cathy wants?'

'Sure she's only a child. She'll soon get used to it and then it'll all be so good for her.' Ellen's voice dropped. She sounded unconvinced even to herself.

'Will I ask her, Jim?'

'Ye might do worse, Sissie.'

'An' what if she says no?'

'Then ye go back, make a life fer yoursel' an' if ye can send fer me, do. An I'll come runnin'. But, if ye can't, well ye can't. I'll understand.'

The church clock struck two and Jim stood up, straightening his trousers and pulling his white apron, now crumpled, out of his pocket. Ellen slid down from the wall fishing the American book, wrapped in brown paper, from beneath her scarf. She passed it to him in silence, then hugged him tightly, feeling the hard bones of him against her.

'Bye Jimmy. If that's the way it's to be, that's the way it's to be. You can be sure we'll be together before much longer. We'll be family in America.'

Chapter 19

Ellen. West Cork: July 1908.

''Tis her we ask, Ellen. And we'll settle this before she goes to bed tonight.'

'I'll meet her, so I will, an' walk her back home, then maybe she'll feel more comfortable with me again. Remember me as her mammy.'

'You can do that, Ellie girl, I've no objection. Now I know this is going to be hard on you, but I'm going to have Michael ask her what she wants when neither of us is with her. If you ask her, she'll be obliged and same goes with me. That's fair enough now, isn't it?'

Ellen's nod suggested approval, but her lips were taut and moved in the opposite direction. She pulled on her coat, avoiding her mother's eye, and fastened the heavy boots she'd borrowed from Nora, in preparation for the long walk.

Mary Clancey watched her daughter leaving the room with a set to her shoulders that she recognised from years of battling. Striding off towards the familiar school route, Ellen muttered objections to herself all the way down the mud-caked lane, thick and slippery with fallen leaves.

She remembered how she had run home from the school many years ago. 'All the children were in small groups, an' I was always friends with the ones I run with. Well today I'll keep Cathy from her friends, she'll have me for company an' I'll be taking my time. There won't be any running. I couldn't help missing the milestone of Cathy's first day at school, I just hope to God I can make up for that.'

Alone behind the school gate, the light flickering out from the schoolroom window wasn't strong enough to let her see the details. The schoolyard itself brought back the excitement of being with other children and the smells, both warm musty human and dry dusty slate chalk. "That room there was my world when I was Cathy's age," she thought, "And I'm grateful. For sure it was the reading and the writing which helped me when I had to get away."

Ellen bit her lip and shivered, facing the realization that this was now Cathy's world, where she was settled and happy. 'Should I really take her from all this?' she murmured, scuffing her boot back and forwards on the dry earth. 'Away from where she is known and secure? Is it selfish to want to move her to live amongst strangers? Will she feel like I felt last week in Dunmanway?'

Ellen pulled her coat closer, and fixed her eyes on the schoolhouse door. It wasn't cold, but a persistent shiver of unease started behind her shoulders and flickered down to her belly.

'Cathy, over here. Cathy.' With a little head of dark curly hair just like Ellen's own, bobbing amongst the group of excited children, her daughter squeezed out the door. She had a slight frame and neat pretty face, and to her mother's relief she bore no likeness to the Berish family.

Cathy's dimples, like thumbprints in putty, appeared on both sides of her cheeks as she saw who was waiting and her cries of 'Sissie! Sissie!' broke a smile onto Ellen's face.

Ellen clutched Cathy's hand, relishing the feel of small warm fingers as they stumbled together over the rough fields, potholed with badger sets and pockmarked by rabbits. There were ditches to jump across and tough hillocks of marshy rushes to squelch through. It took an hour before the gable ends of the farmhouse could be seen.

Ellen was swallowing down the words she'd promised not to say, her good intentions dissolving as fast as their precious journey time. But it was no use, the forbidden questions filled her mouth and she had to let them spill.

'Would ye like to come back to America with me, Cathy? On a big ship, with a cabin all to ourselves and an exciting new world waiting for us on the other side?'

'I would Sissie, really I would.'

Ellen's spirit leapt. She gave a small skip over the nearest hillock, and the drum beat in her heart slowed and settled back into its groove.

'But not until I'm a big girl. I don't want to leave Mammy and Dada now. They would be sad without me. And Michael, Dan and Nora too. And Jimmy of course, he'd miss me. And Mary Anne might have a little baby and I'd be an auntie and she will want me to play with it.'

Ellen took a deep breath, the drum beat speeded up again.

'Well please, darling. Just think about it and when Michael asks you this evening; remember all the good things I told you about, the fun we will have together and the new friends you will make. I'm to be married and maybe we will have a little baby ourselves, then you won't be an auntie, you'll be a big sister. And I'll let you push the perambulator up and down New Jersey sidewalks. Doesn't that sound great?'

She reckoned she'd get away with that afterthought and shrugged away the niggling doubt that at thirty-five another baby was unlikely.

Cathy tilted her head and squinted up at her. The dimples disappeared. Her small face bore a look, which, on an older girl, could have seemed sceptical. The child seemed aware that her replies were important, not only for Ellen but also for herself.

Although she was more tense than she had felt since her negotiations with Uncle Corrie, Ellen swung Cathy's hand in her own. She moved the conversation distractedly onto the first thing she noticed underfoot.

'These rushes, Cathy, do you peel them back and run your fingernail inside the white spongy bit? And in these boggy places, do you like to squelch the soft mud between your toes? I used to do that when I was your age.'

"But I was older than you, so much older," she thought. "The day I sat on that boulder over there, picked at the rushes, and made my plan for you, and I didn't know then how much I would love you, little one." The thoughts remained thoughts and Cathy, seeming to be relieved by the turn of conversation, responded with small-child chirpy answers.

The family meal was ready when they came home, too early for Ellen who had hoped to spend more time alone with her daughter. She had no appetite. Cathy was talkative throughout the meal, telling Mam details of the school day, as a child who is secure and confident about their place at the family's centre would expect to do.

Ellen's shoulders drooped, along with her mood. She wasn't included, an outsider in the circle of attention between grandmother and child.

She watched her mother, thinking how the older woman had changed. When she herself had been a child Mam had been keen to send her out to help with the farm chores. She'd be feeding the hens or collecting the eggs, throwing the slops pail out to the pigs or helping with whatever crop needed to be harvested. There was never any time for herself and her sisters to share news, coming in from school. She could see there was less pressure on her mother these days, which might be why the attention she gave Cathy had never been shown her. Whatever the reason, she could see her daughter was being loved and cared for.

"I should feel relieved, or even grateful, but there's no room in my heart for anything other than a growing dread of the answer," she thought, crumbling her bread, looking way. She distracted herself by scratching an imaginary mark on the table surface, her throat growing more restricted as the conversations continued.

Ellen flitted from chore to chore all evening, finishing nothing she started. First deciding to wipe over the eggs then thought the dishcloths needed rinsing. Out to the pump for fresh water and then in with firewood. She kept looking out of the window, checking for any sign of Michael when she was tidying the washing drying above the fire.

The day was darkening along with her mood when he finally arrived home. As soon as he came in the door his mother pointed to Cathy. 'This child will be goin' to bed soon an' she needs a bit of a conversation with yourself like. You remember?'

'I need to wash an' eat Ma, I'm starved, can it not wait?'

Looking at him with raised eyebrows she nodded towards Ellen whose face was icy pale.

'Right so, Mam.' Michael sighed, knowing no objection would succeed. 'Cathy, we'll have a bit of a walk outside here now, 'tis a lovely evenin' an' I just want to show ye the oul sow. We'll take this lamp with us so.' Lifting the oil lamp off the windowsill he held out his hand to the child. Excited by the offer of a trip out with Michael, she was doing little jumping movements and clapping her hands.

'She's just whelped a litter an' ye should see them now. Ye might want to name one of them yersel' like.'

'Is that what she usually does Michael, or is this something new? Something to make her want to stay? I never remember naming the pigs when I was her age.'

'Oh but I do Sissie; I've named the baby pigs every time. Well, not all, but there is always just one I love and I'll look out for it, the littlest one.'

Although Ellen knew what to expect when her daughter came back into the house, she had to swallow hard to stop from crying. She gripped her arms, wrapping them around her strong solid body. She held her breath watching as her little girl, shaking her head, black curls tumbling over her eyes, gripped onto Michael's hand.

'No. No. No. No. I'm not goin' to Amerikay. I wants to stay here.'

The following morning she took her mother's bicycle and cycled the winding country road into Derryleague. The bright sunshine and profusion of wildflowers glowing in the hedges could not lift her mood. She'd put on her best outfit. The long tweed coat and wide-brimmed velvet hat with the net, the one she'd worn on her visit to Uncle Corrie. It looked unusual as she wobbled and weaved her way into town. She knew it was an unseasonable outfit, but it gave her a morsel of confidence. Ellen held her head high as she approached the Post Office halfway down Main Street.

'Agent Berish, will you take this return ticket and settle me a sailing back to New York as soon as ever ye can? I'll take the steerage class this time, just whatever sailing you can get me, please. And no need to be holding the spare ticket for the child. Plans have changed.'

'Ah, sure I'm sorry to hear that, missus.' The shipping agent leaned across the desk, peering at her with his sharp grey eyes. It didn't look as though he was sorry, more as though he wanted to read into her thoughts. After a moment's silence, he conceded. 'There's been a cancellation the day, Miss Clancey. Some trouble over at the O'Donovans. You might have heard?'

'Yes, well. Plans do change, so there it is. One adult ticket, I've the open return here. Steerage if you please. And I know nothing of the O'Donovans.'

The agent tilted his head and peered again, reminding her

so much of a sparrow looking for crumbs that she thought he might cheep.

She didn't respond, she had nothing to offer, no titbit of gossip. After a moment when neither of them spoke he shrugged his shoulders and, as if bestowing a great favour, said 'I can let you have it, so.' Then, pushing the papers towards her, he explained that the sailing was in two days' time.

'I'll take it then. Thank you, Mister Berish.'

Arriving home that afternoon, she was keen to let the family know all her travel arrangements as quickly as possible. She feared that the pain inside would rupture and overwhelm her if she delayed.

'Michael, Da, can the horse be spared on Wednesday? There's a sailing to New York. Will someone take me in the car?'

'Ah, Sissie, should ye leave so quickly? We've hardly got used to having you around the place an' Jim will want to see you before ye go.'

'Sorry Michael, my mind's made up, so it is. There's one's wanting me in New York, waiting for me. My intended. And the wedding arrangements have to be settled. Then the Rochesters, they will have missed me too. I'm loved there so I am, and I don't want to miss the fine chance of a new life now do I?'

All sense of novelty or anticipation was absent on the voyage back. Steerage class was more cramped than she'd expected, and the communal washing areas, as she'd been warned, became more squalid the further out to sea they sailed.

Ellen lost her appetite, found sleeping difficult and hardly noticed her surroundings. She shared the sense of bewilderment and despair that several of her fellow passengers, most whom were first time voyagers, were displaying. It was slightly comforting to be amongst those whose drooped shoulders, worn clothing and pale anxious faces reflected the way she felt.

When the ship docked at Ellis Island, she was herded

through the registration process, directed to a shorter queue and marked as an 'Immigrant Alien'.

'Do I not need to confirm sponsorship or have a medical?' The uniformed immigration official shrugged his shoulders. A curt wave of his hand told her where to move.

She shuffled through the shorter line, trying not to push against the legs of the people in front.

Ellen yawned, tired and nauseated. She longed for her small room at the top of the Rochesters' house. Once her papers had been stamped she was asked to go down the wide steps of Registration Hall, into the waiting tug. A few minutes took her across the brief stretch of water, past the Statue of Liberty and onto the dockside.

She lifted her head as the tug bumped against the landing stage, her tired eyes seeking the orange-yellow of a New York taxi cab. Although she was reluctant to pay 50 cents a mile, she reckoned there wasn't much to save for anymore.

'Helen, over here. I'm over here.' George's face was flushed beneath a hat she hadn't seen before, a bowler. She gave a small wave and then smiled, recognising his best woollen lounge suit, starched white collar and the peacock blue tie.

Pushing her way towards him, skirting around the placard bearing agents and the clusters of hopeful immigrants surrounding them, her mood began to lighten.

'I've missed you, Helen, I surely have. I only got your letter this morning, that was so lucky. I might not have made it, but here you are. I still can't believe it. And you said you were coming alone? Where is the little girl?'

'It's best she stays with my family, George. They are so fond of her and she of them. I decided it wouldn't be right for me to ask her to give everything up and make a new life here. It near broke my heart, and hers, but we all feel it's for the best.'

Ellen sighed as she handed him her suitcase, confident that this time he would order them a cab. She watched him wave down a smart open carriage car, not a yellow taxicab, and as she stood by the side seeing how he negotiated with the driver, her hope for the future grew stronger.

'I can do this,' she muttered. 'I can build a new life here, a better life. I will be an American wife and stepmother, maybe even a mother again. I'll come through, and he's a good man.'

'Got us one, Helen. A Rockwell. Dandy little vehicle and you'll see more from this height than you would from the yellows.' Seated upright on the leather bench seat of the open-topped taxicab, she pulled the skirt of her coat tightly over her knees. Then she held her hands at chest height and removed her gloves, one finger at a time. She had seen some of Mrs Margaret's friends do that.

George was sitting silent beside her, his cane manly upright between his legs, his gaze focussing on the road ahead.

'These cabs are the ones I prefer,' he told her, without waiting for her question. 'Since you arrived at Battery Quay last time the yellows have become more plentiful and very popular.' Ellen blinked, forcing herself to concentrate. She had never had any interest in vehicles, whether the horse-drawn car her father and Michael used or this precarious machine. She heard him say, 'New owners, this company come down from Baltimore.'

She jolted, suddenly alert. 'Baltimore? 'Tis a fishing harbour where I come from, George. The very same name. Would there be a connection at all?'

'Helen, my dear, everything in America is connected to the old countries, whether it's Ireland, Italy or Israel. We all just accept it, part of us, part of our past, part of our future. And we move on, taking it with us.'

'So it seems. Nothing new, everything linked. And I will move on too, George. I'll make a life with you here, so I will, and accept that my Cathy is now another mother's child.'

Chapter 20

Lizzie. Bristol: May 2023.

Lizzie winced and sipped a mug of bitter, lukewarm coffee. She stepped barefoot over the short distance between her kitchen and the study alcove, looking despairingly at her messy desk.

Wiping her mouth with the back of her hand, she sighed. Eating beans on toast perched on a stool at the kitchen worktop wasn't the glamorous lifestyle she aspired to.

The late afternoon signalled the day nearly over and the promised interview with an emerging television star hadn't materialised. All day and just phone calls with several false leads. Her fatigue grew from a mixture of frustration and boredom.

Begging for a gin and tonic to replace the coffee, her body niggled. She ignored the niggle, the urge to find Ellen was stronger.

Sighing, she shuffled photocopied certificates of people she never knew and would never meet, around on the top of her tiny desk. Some papers had slipped onto the floor. She scrabbled amongst them, like a squirrel in winter, for the elusive nut, a clue which might unearth a new truth.

'Fuck. What is this muddle? Have I missed something I should have been recording? Perhaps I should be concentrating more on the people in my life today. There is a fascination with the past, her past, which is taking over my present. I'm usually slick and organised, but now I seem to be unravelling at the seams.'

She sensed that the untidy room, filled with an accusing silence, would have agreed.

Dumping the handful of papers from the floor onto her desk, she swept her hands back and forth until she found it. The letter from Skibbereen which had arrived in the post that morning. Concentrating on her work calls she had, with uncharacteristic negligence, thrown it in the direction of the desk.

Ripping it open, she pulled out the headed notepaper compliment slip. The Heritage Centre. She'd almost forgotten about the special search. One thing she really needed was the child's birth certificate. No church record seemed to exist with any information about Ellen's baby. She was curious to know more. Why were there two surnames and why did she go to America when her child was about five or six? And did she ever come back?

'OK, so now we have it. Ellen and Patrick, they go to Cork, pretend to be married, have the baby. Big deal. Then at the most six months later, the census took place in April 1901, Ellen and the baby return to her family home. And then she goes to America. Didn't she care about her little girl or what? So many questions. Will I ever know the answer?'

Lizzie rubbed her eyes and yawned as she switched on her computer and ran another search. A few seconds passed and the search found icon appeared.

'Eureka! Here she is again.'

She grabbed her heavy-duty microscope magnifying glass ; it worked more effectively than using the on-screen expand facility. A certificate completed in careful handwriting. A marriage between Helen Clancey and George Clark.

'Yup, Ellie, I know you're Helen now and I can understand why but your date of birth 1881. Really? Surely this is an almost sacred document? Calling for absolute truth. I know it was 1874, Ellie. You just can't keep getting younger. How Rufus would love that, maybe your new husband did too?'

'Hi Lizzie, you can stop talking to yourself now. I'm home!'

Ricocheting against the kitchen wall before landing, Rufus's red and white designer sports bag just missed the alcove corner before docking at Lizzie's feet.

'Want some tea or more coffee, Liz?'

'Hi Rufie. Big glass of red please. Just about at my wits' end with this great-great-grandmother of mine.'

'No! what's she done now? More fibbing? You should see your face; looks like you need a drink!'

'You know what? I no longer care to wonder why, and now she further misleads me.'

'Hang on, Liz. Misleads you! She was dead long before you were born. Whoever she's misleading, it's not personal.'

'But it feels personal. I feel she is part of me now. I care about her and I know she would have cared about me too...'

'Fanciful nonsense! Here, Merlot. OK?'

'Cheers. First today.' Lizzie took a sip, smiled as the warm tannin circled her mouth, then swallowed before continuing.

'Listen to this Rufie, she's given the wrong date of birth, again, even younger than she was on the ship's manifest. Don't smirk like that. No, I wouldn't, you know I wouldn't.'

'Yeah 'course you wouldn't Lizzie, not our Miss goody goody.'

'Seriously Rufus, shuffling through her papers and grabbing the one she needed, she waved it in the air at Rufus. 'She arrived from Queenstown on the ship SS *Coronia*, in 1906.'

'Bloody Hell, you know what? That woman did have some luck somewhere in her life. That ship was wrecked, I was reading about it that time you asked me to help with the search. I made a note, it's on my tablet. Here, take a look.'

'Rufus, I can't believe you did that, you've got a whole file going there, let me see. What do you call it?'

'Lizzie's Bear Hunt.'

'What a star you are! What've you got for me then?'

'Well, in March 1907 there was a crew of thirty and one hundred and twenty four passengers. Now if that was a cruise ship today they would have about ninety crew members to that number of passengers. I know it wasn't a fancy cruise ship, but still, that's a very low number of crew.' Rufus took a gulp from his wine glass before continuing.

'Anyway, it ran aground due to a storm. There was only one fatality. Which I know isn't awful, but it must have been very scary, so she dodged that one.'

'Well, you know I didn't really mean to judge her harshly. Sorry, Ellen. And since Faith and I went to Ellis Island I've realised more about what it was like, the ships, the uncertainty, everything.'

'I'd say it was tough enough. Now come on over here and let me show you my etchings. I had a shower at the club, by the way.'

Lizzie sipped her wine and looked longingly at her own computer screen, before flicking the switch. Swivelling her chair around to face Rufus, whose lanky frame was now spread out across the floor, she lifted his empty wine glass. His attention was still hovering over the tablet flickering on his lap.

'I wonder what she would say if she could see us, Rufie? What a gap there is between her life and ours. Do you think she had choices, who to love and how to love?'

'You shouldn't be so hard on her, Liz. You've really no idea what it was like. But speaking of love, now must I ask you again? Come here and let me see whether you've inherited even a bit of her adventurous spirit!'

Chapter 21

Lizzie. Bristol: October 2023.

Lizzie sighed. Her mind whirled, flitting over and back across a decision she had to make. She didn't want advice but without having someone to talk to she wasn't getting anywhere, and the days were slipping by.

She thought about talking it through with her sister. Their trip to New York six months ago had brought them close and now they shared confidences. "Just like proper sisters" was how Lizzie described their reenergised relationship.

She smiled, recalling the effort she'd had to make to wring information out of Faith. It reminded her of squeezing lemons. Even when she'd taken the tightest grip and persisted longer than she should have, her sister had released just a few drops. The man friend. Another squeeze and his name was Martin. 'Ah, at last, the pip!' and, then, apart from the scant details she'd been told at the airport, nothing more. Now, without warning, she'd said they were planning a visit to Bristol.

Lizzie knew that everything with Faith was planned. Although she threw her clothes about as if she didn't care, beneath that facade was a very structured person. She was confident that her sister's advice would be sound and considered. They were arriving at the weekend and Rufus was picking them up. He had offered to take Martin on a tour of the city, giving her some time alone with Faith. There were landmarks which Rufus had been planning on photographing for months. She hoped Martin would be patient.

Still in her pyjamas, she wandered around the kitchen collecting odd utensils and mugs which were scattered across the surfaces.

'I'm calling in sick, Rufie. I need to sort some stuff out and there aren't any celebrities clamouring at my door today.'

'You do look a bit peaked, Liz, go back to bed. I'll be late home tonight. Got a badminton challenge to win. Probs nineish. Have a good day.'

A backwash of aftershave and men's cologne surrounded her as Rufus blew her a kiss, before smashing out the door with his briefcase and sports bag.

Pulling one of Rufus's hoodies over her pyjamas, she padded across the kitchen floor to the laptop, its screen light beckoning. 'Perhaps,' she told herself, 'perhaps I am becoming obsessed with this online search for Ellen. Perhaps I should just content myself with knowing she left Ireland, gave up her baby and emigrated to America.'

Lizzie rubbed her back and considered whether to go for a shower or return to bed, but the online searching results were good so far and she persuaded herself that another hour might just do the trick.

'Such an encouraging success last week, discovering that marriage certificate, and then, hearing from that relative in West Cork, who thought Ellen had had a second child, George, born in America. Although I'd been told he only lived a few months, so how can they be sure of family memory so long ago?'

Clicking onto the search site, she keyed in the details. Five minutes of scrolling found the information. 'Dear God, was there nothing about Ellen's life that turned out right?'

Her stomach churned, she felt the rise in the back of her throat, and the familiar watery sensation in her mouth, an urgent precursor to a vomit. Rushing across the floor, she retched over the toilet bowl, tears choking and bile filling her mouth with acid. Pulling her hair back into an unsecured bun, she wiped the side of her hand across her face. Leaning against the wall she rocked back on her heels, crying and sweating.

'Why, baby, why did it happen? Was she an unfit mother? Abandoning one child and then allowing another one to die. She seemed so brave, leaving everyone she knew and making a new life for herself on another continent. But after all that, perhaps she was just plain careless?'

Dragging herself up from the floor, she wiped her face, flushed the toilet and leaned over the sink, looking for mouthwash. Pulling open the bathroom cabinet and moving her wash bag to one side reminded her of its contents. She needed to do something about them.

Lizzie groaned as she looked again at the thin red line on the pregnancy test. 'If I tell him, then it's not my choice anymore. If I don't tell him soon, he'll think I've been hiding it from him and I don't want to do that either. Just the timing never seems right. Well, one thing is for sure, I can choose. I have enough money, a job and a future. That's a lot more than poor old Ellen had.'

Although her guts hadn't stilled she managed a weak grin, reminding herself that her situation wasn't in any way like Ellen's. That being unmarried wasn't the same as being alone, disgraced or expected to keep secret the knowledge that her child was illegitimate.

Options flitted across her mind. She did love Rufus and was pretty sure she could stay with him. But if he wasn't ready to be a grown-up yet, she would have to leave him. She could easily maintain the child on her own, or she could co-parent. She could even, maybe, have an abortion. No. That simply wasn't going to happen. She couldn't, wouldn't, let herself imagine the pain of having to give a child away.

Swilling out her mouth with the peppermint wash, she spat angrily into the sink. The mirror reflected a pale scared face, hair secured back apart from a few lank tendrils falling across her cheek. 'I'm being stupid,' she nodded towards the girl in the mirror who seemed to agree. 'I'm actually on the verge of a new and exciting chapter in my life. And maybe with a new life. Should I really spend any more time delving into Ellen Clancey's?'

Stripping off the hoodie, Lizzie let her pyjamas drop to the floor as she stepped into the shower. Hot water cascaded over her, cleansing her sticky body.

Shaking her hair and wrapped in clean bath towels, she felt her body relax, responding to her calmed emotions, nudging her to eat.

Tea and a slice of toast were all she could manage. She turned back to the computer, its quiet humming beckoned.

Two clicks found baby Clark's death certificate. Ten weeks after his birth. One hundred and thirteen years had passed, but seeing the certificate made it feel like a recent heartbreak. Her eyes blurred, scanning the details.

'Hello, hello. Here we have an elegant script, firm and confident, an educated hand. It has recorded forever the last and possibly only detail of this child's life. Cause of death: Gastro Enteritis. Oh, and some more. Seems like the same doctor had attended the child four days before he died. The same name was on the birth certificate. Well, what do you reckon? He was known to the family, someone readily available. Why couldn't he have helped more?'

She shut down the computer with shaking hands and called out to her long dead great-great-grandmother, 'How on earth have you let this happen? Dirty hands, dirty bottle, unsafe water, what were you thinking Ellen? I've followed your journey all these months. I'd grown to like you, love you even. Now it's all gone.'

She considered creeping back to bed when the green blink signalling mobile phone message distracted her. It was an American relative. She'd known Jimmy had emigrated, following Ellen, and this man was his grandson. She'd first heard from him a year ago, just after her visit to Derryleague.

Her mind wandered to their last conversation. It had surprised him to learn of Cathy's existence and it had surprised Lizzie to learn that it hadn't been known. Neither Ellen nor James told anyone in America. She reckoned that was sad. Jim and Ellen lived long and close lives in New Jersey, the American had assured her. He implied that her marriage had been a loving and stable one. He'd also told her Ellen had been a good stepmother to George's son, Thomas.

Opening the email she found a brief greeting. 'Hi Lizzie, Here's an interview me and my brother had last week, with our uncle, one of Jim's sons.' An audio was attached.

Pushing some loose papers from the couch onto the floor, she nestled herself into the cushions. Lodging the remains of her plate of toast onto the arm of the sofa, she clicked open the recording.

Soon she was giggling; eavesdropping on another world. It was a different culture, but still the same sense of humour. It was one she recognised as old Joe's, filtering through. The banter was fast flowing, describing long-ago events as though they had been recent occurrences. The old man was talking like she imagined an Irish- American gangster might. Every now and again he'd interject between the brothers, 'You're a good guy' before revising his earlier opinion. 'Compared to some. Well on a scale…'

'This old guy is merciless,' she muttered through crunched remnants of toast. 'Wow, just listening to this, all the paper research is coming to life. I can get a better sense of who they were, and they were fun people. Thank God! I was despairing of there being any fun at all in this clan of mine.' Stretching her legs out for a break, Lizzie pressed the pause button.

'I'm thinking,' she shook her damp hair, running her finger through the tangles. 'I'm thinking that this family has a sense of humour. They are realistic and don't seem to expect too much but accept one another for who and what they are. Oh Ellie, they surely did love you in America. You, with your brand-new husband, stepson and brother. Were you the start of something special? I do hope so. This hasn't half cheered me up!'

Switching the audio back on again, she heard the brothers being reminded of the time they returned from Ireland as young teenagers, proud of their Arran knit sweaters. "Chain link" their uncle called them. 'An' you wore them inside out. You looked like shaggy sheep, we never told you, and you wore them all winter like that.'

She closed her eyes, transported to another time, another continent. Bristol and West Cork faded as she learned more about the lives of relatives she'd never known.

'Well, what d'ye know? Here's this one character "on the form," it sounds like a type of witness protection! A bootlegger, eh? From the old prohibition days when he was producing whiskey and stout. Glamour. Bonny and Clyde eat your heart out. Here come the Clanceys.'

The fledgling hope which had hatched in her began to grow stronger. She learned that the two countries were much more familiar with each other than she'd expected. They discussed a little Irish grotto, in a place Lizzie had never heard of, called 'Inchingeelagh', as though it were a local New Jersey landmark.

'The more I hear of these little gems, these snippets they've sent me, the better I see how the lives of Irish migrant families overlapped.'

And 'What about that!' she exclaimed, hearing that a neighbour from "two fields away" who emigrated shortly before Jim was the one who got him a job.

As the recording continued to describe a mix of people integrating while also keeping within their own community, she giggled. 'It's like all I had was the road map, but it couldn't show me the gradient or the terrain of the route itself. Thanks, Jim's son, I'm viewing in technicolour now!'

She stopped the recording and walked to the window, leaning on the sill and looking down onto her street. 'Here it is, the ever changing but staying the same pattern. The drifting, scurrying, backpack carrying, dogwalking, everyday life. Same as it ever was.

'That song, didn't they say you may find yourself living in another part of the world? Talking Heads, I'm sure.' Turning back into the room she played the last few minutes of the recording. 'And it seems like Ellen did find herself and was surrounded by people who were fun and brave and sometimes a bit crazy too.'

The men were getting to the end of their reminiscences and Lizzie wanted to make sure she caught all the nuances of her American ancestors' lives.

'But this lot are confused,' she muttered, hearing the men mixing up the identities of several members of the original Clancey family. 'And goodness, they're calling Henley-on-Thames Temley-on-Hames! Bloody hilarious! But to be fair, I don't even know where Inchingeelagh is, I'll have to look it up. I'll just enjoy the insight they have given me and take it for what it is. Well, I guess it's all part of my family too.'

Lizzie switched off the recording and smiled as she put her hand on her stomach. 'Just like you, another little descendent.'

As she crawled into bed, her ache of disappointment for Ellen's baby lessened by what she had just learned. She fell asleep curving her hands around where she thought her own baby might be.

Rufus face was partly visible in the grey evening light, as he crouched down beside the bed, his hand on her shoulder.

'You can put the light on Rufus, I'm getting up now.'

'Lizzie, kiddo, what's going on? You still not well?'

'I'm well enough Rufie, just tired.'

Squinting with the bright overhead light, Lizzie plunged in. 'We're going to have a baby.'

Several emotions seemed to flicker across Rufus's face. She could usually tell from his eyes and shoulders, but this time he gave no hints. She wriggled her back further up the bed, hoping to see him better from a closer angle.

For a moment or two, neither of them spoke. The announcement hung in the air, suspended. The words in-vitro came to Lizzie's mind. Her baby, their baby, its future suspended along with their relationship.

'When did you find out, Liz? I thought the implant was almost foolproof?'

'I did too. But I forgot to get it renewed. Anyway Rufus, you don't need to worry.' Lizzie gulped, trying to sound convincing. 'I can do this on my own if you don't want me.'

'Lizzie, are you daft? Of course you're not doing it on your own. Who do you think you are, Ellen Clancey?'

'Ah no, Rufie. I'm so upset for her. She had a baby; it died after ten weeks, Gastro Enteritis. I just hope it wasn't neglect. But listen, I got this tape recording...'

'Nooo, don't be ridiculous, of course it wasn't neglect. Don't always jump to conclusions. There will have been a reason, a good reason. But now I want to talk about our baby, and you. Us.'

Lizzie breathed out, deep and slow. 'You do want the baby then, Rufus? Looks like there is a lot more for me than Ellen ever had.'

Pulling back the duvet, she smiled and moved over in the bed. 'Hop in then, you great white sweaty one and keep me warm while we make plans.'

Rufus stumbled over the legs of his tracksuit as he pulled the sports pants down and climbed in beside her.

Chapter 22

Lizzie and Rufus. Bristol: October 2023.

The flight bringing Faith and Martin into Bristol airport was due to arrive at midday and Rufus was going to pick them up. Wearing his favourite smart casual wear – designer jeans, crisp white shirt over navy statement tee – he looked like someone who had dressed to impress.

Lizzie felt a buzz of pride as she surveyed him head to toe. She'd spent most of the morning in a bath with some expensive skin products and was giving her makeup a final touch as she waited for the coffee. While the percolator popped and spluttered, she turned to Rufus.

'I'm still bewildered by the baby death. How could they be so unlucky? I know infant mortality in those days was high but I hope she wasn't careless. She wasn't, was she Rufus?'

'And what were their living conditions like?' Rufus slurred through a mouthful of Weetabix and power seeds.

Lizzie turned the percolator off and poured two small cups before replying in a voice which was dragging out reluctant words.

'Well, they were living in a tenement house, multi-occupied. At least they were in the 1910 census so maybe the conditions were so bad she couldn't help it. I dunno. I'm conflicted, Rufie.'

Hearing the sadness in her voice, Rufus put an encouraging arm around her shoulders.

'A girl torn away from her baby,' Lizzie said. 'Encouraged, if not persuaded, to leave the child with her family to be raised as their own daughter? The poor woman. But on the other hand, why did she never come back for the child when she got married and had a home to offer?'

'Look Liz, I'm not due to leave for at least half an hour yet. I'm just going to Google Earth it now. Give me the address again.'

Pushing his cereal bowl to one side, Rufus pulled the laptop closer.

'Stand back Lizzie, I'm going in.'

'Budge up then Rufie, let me see.' Lizzie's hair fell forward over her face and Rufus absentmindedly stroked the back of her neck whilst moving the cursor around the screen with his other hand.

She shivered, watching the cursor zoom across the world from their apartment in Bristol to the house in New Jersey.

'Is this the house which Ellen, or Helen, or Ellie, or Sissie called home? I can almost feel the centuries melt away as the cursor is swooping down, hovering above the image of this house.'

Lizzie pushed closer, sucking a damp tendril of hair, straining to make out the details.

'Magic isn't it, Liz? How George would have loved this Google Earth! It looks enormous. A very dignified house for sure. I remember the census lists fifty people living at that address. That does include her and George, all sharing accommodation.'

'Fifty seems unlikely, Rufus. Can it be right?'

'Hard to know, really, I can't quite understand the census record, but it does look like it. They had to do what they could. Her brother Jimmy wasn't there until a few years later was he? Didn't you find him in the 1920 census with young Thomas, George's son. You mustn't judge her Liz, she will have done her best.'

'I know. I'm sure she really did do her best to survive, Rufie.

Remember how she claimed to be twenty-nine when she was in fact thirty-six? A much better marriageable proposition. I expect she knew she hadn't too much time left before there'd be no chance for another child.'

'Numbers weren't her strong suit were they, Liz?'

'You're right, of course you are. And how about her husband too? Widowed and then loses the child. Two deaths within a few years.'

'But remember, you know, all what they told you, those American rellies of yours?' Rufus closed the laptop and turned to her, taking her face in both hands. 'He was fun, that George, with his magic tricks, they loved visiting as kids. She was happy with him and a loving step-mum too. They were a real family after all the trauma and tragedy.'

Lizzie pulled his hands away, leaning into his shoulder. 'I'm still conflicted, Rufus. Was she a good woman, a loving caring woman who was dealt a poor hand? If so, did she make the best of it, or was she a hard selfish woman only looking out for herself? Did she love her kid, did her kid resent her or what?'

'Lizzie, Liz, you might never know. And whatever that house might look like now, it was definitely multi-occupied. They would not have had much space to themselves. All facilities would have been shared too. Probably had an outside toilet and so the conditions of raising a newborn would not have been what you and I are going to have.'

Lizzie stood up suddenly, pulling away from Rufus. Her eyes were wide, her bottom lip quivering.

'What is it Liz, have you seen a ghost?'

'For crying out loud. I forgot to tell you Rufus. There is something I've always known, and now I can't believe how I could have overlooked it. One of my great-granny's daughters was called Ellen. Cathy called her oldest daughter Ellen.'

'Whaat? Jesus wept, Liz. You telling me now after all this

soul searching?' Rufus shook his head but his faint smile reassured her.

'You keep on asking about was Cathy happy, how much feeling did she have for her real mother? And you want to know what was Ellen really like, was she a hard woman or a kind one? Then all along you knew Cathy named one of her daughters after her mother in America?'

'Well yes, it does seem stupid of me, sorry. I'd forgotten all this mishmash of internet searching. What a dumbass! Her first child, so I guess Cathy must have loved Ellen and not had any bad feeling about not being taken to America. Maybe they kept in touch...'

'Exactly! Would you, in a million years, call your child after someone you had had a bad experience with?'

'Never, no, never. It was staring me right in the face all along. Now that is family love seeping down through the generations, isn't it Rufus?'

'Liz, you and me, we are going to have our own family to look after now. It's all anyone can do at the end of the day. They did their best, we will do our best. No two families are the same anyway.'

Rufus checked his watch, needing to leave. He kissed Lizzie on the top of her head.

'I'll have my camera out all the way along, you'll be sourcing pony riding lessons for kids. We'll argue a lot. I won't expect you to do what I want you to do and I'll probably be a selfish bastard sometimes. But that's life, we will both be fine with that. We don't need to get married to be a family, we'll just be us. With a baby. You know?'

'Let's go out tonight, Rufie. Out for dinner, my treat.'

'Sudden improvement, eh? Some bits of you never change do they? I reckon we should check first with Faith and Martin, see what they want to do. No?'

Rufus reached for his jacket and camera. 'Time to go Liz,

put some clothes on before we get back, will you? Can't have a pregnant woman lolling about half naked when her visitors arrive.'

'Pregnant woman! I never thought of myself like that until now. We are going to be such our own kind of family. Yay! Aunty Faith. I haven't told her yet, and she'll be so chuffed.

'I've no idea what our future holds, but that's the end of the search for me now. I think Granny would be happy with this. The whole point was to find her family, solve the mystery, fill in the missing link. Well, we've done that, and more.'

'And you know what Liz, if this baby is a girl I've a notion we might be calling her Ellie.'

About the Author

Mary is the author of two earlier novels 'Long Road, Many Turnings' and 'Time for a Change'. She is also a prizewinner of the 2020 Fish flash fiction competition. Now living in Devon she describes herself as a hybrid Irish-European. Born and brought up in Northern Ireland, her grandmother's family originate in West Cork, which is the setting of *Another Mother's Child*. Her career as a Midwife and Health Visitor as well as her fascination with people has enriched her writing. Mary hopes her novels generate an understanding of how different characters respond to their life challenges, stimulating a reaction in readers which touches their own feelings and experiences. Although her feet are planted in England her mind is constantly travelling elsewhere, often to the irritation of those who have to live with her. Find out more about Mary at http://marymcclareyauthor. co.uk.

Acknowledgements & Author's note:

'Another Mother's Child' is a work of fiction but as my grandmother used to tell me 'there is nothing original in this world, dearie.' Whether the internet might have persuaded her otherwise we will never know. Much of Ellen's story is as authentic as was feasible and has been researched to reflect the experiences of Irish-American immigrants at the beginning of the twentieth century. So many generous people helped with background and details but I am particularly grateful for the contribution of the following, who gave willingly of their time and knowledge. Barry and Margaret Deane, Diarmuid O'Sullivan, Maura Wilson, Dan Callahan. In addition Chris Frame (Maritime author) for details of the Cunard line as well as the Skibbereen Heritage Centre for their painstaking research and patience. Finally,to West Cork, for being simply beautiful.

Printed in Great Britain
by Amazon